Rachel

Ten Minus Nine Equals
JOANIE

Ten Minus Nine Equals
JOANIE

CLARICE PONT

Illustrated by Lois Maloy

GOLDEN GATE JUNIOR BOOKS • San Carlos, California

FOR CHRISTOPHER, MARK AND ANNE

Ten Minus Nine Equals
JOANIE

ONE

"PLEASE, DADDY, COULDN'T I stay home from school just this once?" Joanie Sanders turned big blue eyes to her father's face towering above her and expressing a mixture of impatience and seriousness.

"No, Joanie, I think not. Your grades this year forbid any unnecessary absences. I'm sorry."

Joanie pushed out her lower lip and said resentfully, "You're staying home! And I should think the high school needs its teacher more than the grade school needs me — "

"Right! But not more than you need the grade school, I'm afraid. Now please don't be difficult, Joanie. There isn't time for it and I have already said no."

Joanie felt it wiser not to pursue the matter. Her indifference to lessons was something she preferred not to discuss for it usually ended in tears and scoldings. Today, at least, everyone ought to be happy, even though Daddy was, after all, about to take Mother to the hospital. Besides, when Daddy said no, in that tone of voice, he meant it. So she shrugged herself into her red jacket and said, "Well, anyway, you *will* name the baby Gwendolyn, won't you? It's such a pretty name,

don't you think?"

"Very pretty. But — oh well, we'll see." Daddy was looking towards the hall where Mother had just stopped to put a note under the milk bottle. Mr. Sanders laughed and went to join her, picking up the small bag on the floor beside her. "How can you think of the extra pound of butter at a time like this!" he said, not questioning so much as exclaiming.

Mrs. Sanders looked as though she found it rather difficult to smile at the moment, but she managed it and said to Joanie, " 'Bye, darling. And do be a good girl for Mrs. Singer. And go straight to her house from school. Daddy will pick you up there just as soon as he is able." Then, turning to her husband again, she said, "Let's go, Roger."

The three hurried to the car which Mr. Sanders had

4

already driven out of the garage. Joanie kissed her parents good-bye, then hurried down to the corner where the school bus would pick her up. She was just in time and she boarded it reluctantly. From the window she could see her father pulling out of their driveway. She waved as he picked up speed.

The children were noisy as usual and Joanie found it a little difficult to keep her thoughts on what was uppermost in her mind. Just imagine, by tomorrow she would be someone's sister! And she would have a sister too! Could anything be more wonderful to think about than that? The fifteen minutes it took to reach school seemed to pass very quickly. She could scarcely believe it when the mad clamor to alight from the bus began. She seemed to float along with the others and somehow, a little later, she found herself sitting at her desk with another routine school day getting under way. Routine? Perhaps that was the way it was for the others. As for Joanie, it was even more difficult than usual for her to concentrate on what Miss Perkins had to say.

Joanie didn't actually dislike learning. It was simply that there always seemed to be so many other things a lot more interesting to occupy her attention. Like the red-breasted robin suddenly bursting into song just outside the schoolroom window. Or the bold, buzzing bluebottle grumbling about the heat. The humming of bees searching flower beds for honey reminded her of the little verse her mother had taught her:

> A sad little girl sat under a tree,
> "Oh, what can I do to be gay?" asked she.
> "Bee bizzee, bee bizzee, bee bizzee,"
> Answered the bumble bee.

And today, besides the anticipation of the new baby sister, there was the beautiful color of Miss Perkins' new blouse. Just like a freshly-cut-into watermelon. *Um-m!* How she loved watermelon! Soon some would be appearing in the markets. Then, added to all these lovely things and thoughts, there was the stingy-sweet scent of the orange blossoms coming from the groves across the street. Five times six was always the same, but all these other things — they were wonderful and exciting and much more interesting to think about.

"Joanie, *please!* If you don't pay better attention I shall have to keep you in at recess. Three times I have asked you a question and all you do is smile over some private little matter of your own." Miss Perkins sounded very annoyed.

"Oh! Oh, I'm sorry, Miss Perkins. But it really isn't private. I'll tell you, if you like. I mean, may I tell the class? It's the loveliest thing — " Joanie's eyes shone brightly and she added, as an afterthought, hoping to make Miss Perkins' frown disappear, "Your new blouse is so pretty."

Miss Perkins bit her upper lip and said, "Thank you."

Then Joanie rushed on, lest she be denied the privilege, "I'm to get a baby sister today!"

The teacher's lips slid apart as though a zipper had released them and she smiled at Joanie. "Well, in that case, I think we can excuse the inattention — but just this once!"

Mary Collins' hand shot up. "Miss Perkins, is Joanie's mamma going to adopt a baby girl?" she asked.

Joanie answered. "Oh, no. This is a for-real sister,

Mary. My mother went to the hospital this morning and — "

Miss Perkins' authority forgotten, Mary spoke directly to Joanie. "Then how can you know it'll be a sister?" she asked. "We didn't know about mine until after she was born. No one does." She was smiling in an irritating manner.

Miss Perkins nodded her head and said, "Mary does have a point there, Joanie. It might very well be a baby brother."

At this suggestion, Joanie felt that familiar tightening in her chest. She felt her face grow warm and red and she exclaimed in a loud voice, "No! It can't be a boy! It just has to be a girl, Miss Perkins. Boys put frogs in your lunch box and they laugh at you and they — " Her face crinkled toward tears at the very memory of an unhappy experience way back in First Grade.

She heard one of the boys mutter, "Sour grapes, I bet. Just sorry 'cause she happens to be a girl herself. Who could really *want* to be a girl? But she doesn't have to wish it on someone else, does she? That just shows you!"

"Perhaps we'd better get back to our lesson," Miss Perkins suggested, asking Joanie if she would please spell the word *thought* for them. Joanie obliged, doing so correctly, but Mary's awful comment still rankled and she felt shaken.

At recess the boys seemed to think they must put Joanie back in her place, squealing such remarks as, "Sugar an' spice an' fat little mice!" One boy went so far as to express the hope the new baby would be twin boys. "Haw! Haw! Haw!" But to offset the hurt, a few of the girls expressed genuine envy of Joanie. Mary Collins said kindly, "I didn't intend to be mean, Joanie. If you want a sister so badly, I do hope you get one."

Joanie's place in the limelight served to cheer her somewhat and when, at the end of the school day, she raced off to Mrs. Singer's house, she was in excellent spirits.

Mrs. Singer was an elderly lady who lived alone. She served her community by growing lovely flowers which she gave proudly to the hospital and church, and by baby-sitting. Joanie could never understand why it should be called baby-sitting when some of the children Mrs. Singer cared for were no longer babies, like herself, for instance. And Mrs. Singer didn't "sit." She was forever bustling around, doing all sorts of things, from washing dishes to playing ring-around-the-rosy with her younger charges.

"Would you like to play in the back garden for a while, Joanie?" Mrs. Singer asked, when Joanie arrived.

"Haven't you heard from my daddy yet?" Joanie asked.

"Not yet. It may be some time, you know."

"Then maybe I'd better get my homework done," Joanie decided, thinking that once her father came there would be too much excitement for her to think of doing homework.

"That's a good idea, Joanie. You may use the back bedroom. It's nice and quiet in there and there's the little desk, too, for you to work at," Mrs. Singer said.

It wasn't easy to concentrate on the homework and it took twice as long as it should have to complete. But finally Joanie closed her books and sought out Mrs.

Singer once more. She hadn't heard the telephone ring, but still she asked, once she had located Mrs. Singer, "Did you hear anything yet?"

Mrs. Singer smiled as she cut up some meat for beef stew. "Not yet, child. Goodness, you *are* anxious about this baby, aren't you? Well, I suppose we just have to be patient. I hope you like stew, Joanie. I put lots of carrots in mine, fresh from the garden, you know. And peas and tiny onions. How was school today?" Mrs. Singer had a startling habit of jumping from one topic to another without warning. But then the telephone rang and she hurried off to answer.

Joanie's heart began beating in excitement, but the call proved to be just one of several requests for Mrs. Singer to baby-sit. Joanie had to resign herself to the fact that her father was not likely to call for her before dinner. It wasn't that Joanie disliked stew, but it would have been so much more fun had he gotten home in time for the two of them to eat dinner together at their own table. They could have talked about the baby while they ate. This was what she had dreamed of all day long. But Mrs. Singer seemed so pleased to have company for dinner and Joanie was, after all, a polite child. "I love stew," she said, bringing a warm smile to the woman's face.

Joanie discovered she was hungry, once she had filled her plate and begun to eat the truly delicious stew. There were hot biscuits, too, fluffy and golden, served with honey and butter. A crisp salad, topped with her favorite dressing, completed the meal except for a luscious-looking apple pie.

"You must be very excited about the baby." Mrs.

9

Singer made conversation as she helped herself to a biscuit.

"Oh yes!" Joanie said. "I've always wanted a little sister. And I love tiny babies. I shall pretend she's a doll who can cry and wriggle and smile without having to be wound up or anything."

"Yes. But suppose — " began Mrs. Singer, with an indulgent smile, all the while spreading butter on her biscuit.

Joanie sensed what was coming. She interrupted hastily, "It's going to be a girl, Mrs. Singer. I know it is."

"Well now, I think that is very trusting of you. But we can't always be absolutely sure, and I wouldn't want to see you — " Mrs. Singer sounded gentle and kind but still managed to stir Joanie's resentment.

"I've even chosen a name for her," Joanie interrupted.

"Really? What is it?"

"Gwendolyn," Joanie proudly replied.

"It's a very lovely name, I must say," said Mrs. Singer. "Won't you have some more honey? Or would you rather save room for the apple pie? I thought we might eat it with your father, if he comes along soon. It's still very hot — "

"Oh, I'll save room, if you don't mind. I love apple pie." Joanie took a drink of milk and dabbed at her lips with her napkin.

The telephone rang again and, as usual, Mrs. Singer jumped up promptly and hurried off to answer it. She was like a jack-in-the-box, in a way, Joanie thought, wanting to giggle. But instead, she pricked up her ears in hopes that this time it would be Daddy. It was!

She heard Mrs. Singer exclaim, "It is? Well, well, how wonderful for you, Mr. Sanders! Congratulations! I'm so happy for you . . . Oh, really? How lovely! — Joanie? Oh, she's fine, just finishing dinner, so don't you worry. Oh yes, I will! She will be so pleased it's here at last — so excited, she is. Oh well, *that!* I'm sure it won't — after all — Well, so long for now, and give my love to Mrs. Sanders, won't you? 'Bye, now —"

Mrs. Singer returned to the table, her kindly face beaming. "Joanie, dear, you have a darling little brother! Eight pounds, five ounces! Isn't that wonderful?"

Joanie choked. Mrs. Singer had to slap her quite hard on the back several times before she could get her breath. Then she drank a whole glass of water and wiped her eyes. She finally looked at Mrs. Singer in disbelief as she asked, haltingly, "D-did you s-say a little b-brother?"

"Yes, dear. Eight pounds, five ounces! Aren't you the lucky one!" Mrs. Singer couldn't have been more delighted, Joanie thought miserably, if someone had just given her a huge box of candy.

Joanie wanted to tell her to stop smiling, to stop acting as if eight pounds, five ounces was the most important thing in the world. Eight pounds, five ounces of boy! Oh, couldn't Mrs. Singer see how hurt Joanie was? Why, this was like opening a Christmas package and finding nothing but an old pair of shoes inside! Couldn't the woman *see?* Suddenly, Joanie was crying.

"Why, Joanie dear, I had no idea it mattered that much to you! A baby's a baby, when all's said and done. They are all just as sweet as can be, you know. I sit for baby boys as well as for baby girls, and I never yet could decide which are the dearest. It always seems like it's the one I'm taking care of at the moment. Just you wait till you see him and — "

"I won't take him! I won't! I wanted a sister! How can you name a boy Gwendolyn, anyway? Daddy must be mistaken, Mrs. Singer, he must!" Joanie choked between sobs.

Mrs. Singer smiled, but there was a little sadness in her smile. Still, she tried to sound cheerful as she said, "Well now, that would sound rather odd, wouldn't it? Of course, there isn't any law forbidding it, as I can recall. As a matter of fact, I once knew a boy named Sharon, but I always felt very sorry for him. It would be like calling you John Henry and I'm sure you wouldn't like that, would you?"

If she'd just stop trying to be funny! Joanie clenched her fists. She wanted to hit out at someone. Not Mrs. Singer, exactly. It wasn't her fault. Still, she needn't be so pleased. Oh, it was cruel! The tears flowed freely again and Mrs. Singer wisely kept still. Presently she remembered the pie and thought it might be cool enough to eat.

"We can have a piece of pie, anyway. I don't think your daddy will mind if we don't wait for him."

As if she thought a piece of pie would cure everything — ! Joanie accepted some, however, and politely tried to eat it. After a while she asked, hopefully, "Mrs. Singer, do you think there might be someone who got a little girl who would rather have a boy? 'Cause, if so, maybe we could exchange! Daddy and Mother know how much I want a sister."

"Well now, I suppose that is something only your

parents can answer. And speaking of angels — here comes your daddy!" Mrs. Singer hurried off to the front door and welcomed Mr. Sanders into the house.

Almost reluctantly, Joanie came towards him. He looked so happy! The kiss he planted on Joanie's cheek was one of joy, but somehow it seemed like a sting to her. She was glad he didn't wait for her to kiss him back. Glad, yes, in a way, because she didn't feel like kissing him just now. But did he have to turn from her so abruptly to begin telling Mrs. Singer that the baby's hair was red as autumn leaves? Oh, she was probably included in the talk, but she had never felt less important and she thought if she left the room she would never be missed. She maintained a stiff silence.

Mrs. Singer cut a huge wedge of pie for Mr. Sanders, and poured freshly-brewed coffee, bidding him pull up a chair to the table to "have a bite."

He ate the pie with obvious enjoyment. In fact, Joanie thought, he looked as if he would enjoy anything right now. His eyes were shining and he kept rubbing his hands together, as she'd seen him do so often when the team he coached at the high school won a game. The piece of pie disposed of, Mr. Sanders rose from his chair and declared they must be going. He grinned across at Joanie as he said, "How about it, Joanie? By golly, did you ever expect to have a little red-haired brother? Hair just like I remember my father's used to be. And, boy, does he have a pair of lungs! You should have heard — "

"Grandfather doesn't have any hair, Daddy," Joanie reminded her father, starting to get her jacket.

"Well, no, not any more, I grant you. He has a bit left, but it isn't red now, of course." He glanced at his watch and added, "Getting late, sweetie-pie. We must get going." He turned to thank Mrs. Singer while Joanie got her jacket and put it on. Red. Red like the baby's hair. Why on earth had she ever wanted a red jacket? Blue was a lot prettier and — and — well, no one could have blue hair!

She felt her father's hand upon her head and heard him say, "A robust little redhead, by golly! How about that, Princess?"

"You said that once," she muttered, keeping her head down. Red hair. Red hair! Boys with red hair were the very worst kind. That boy with the frog — *his* hair had been red. It had looked like rusty, curled-up wire. And his face had been covered with freckles. She'd been so glad when his family moved away. She drew away from her father and opened the door herself. She walked toward the car in silence, not so much a sulky silence as a crushed one.

Her father didn't seem to notice that she sat hunched up tight against the other end of the seat or that she said not a word the entire trip home. She had never felt so lonely in all her life.

But when he went to tuck her in her bed and turn down the light — taking Mother's place as best he could — he finally seemed to realize a little of what she was feeling. It may have been because she turned her face away when he stooped to kiss her, of course. "Joanie," he said softly, "is it that bad, darling? Don't think I don't know you are disappointed. I just thought, if I told you how wonderful the little chap really is, you'd soon forget you had hoped for a girl. Just so long as we have a baby — " He smoothed her hair back and smiled

14

gently. "After all, boy babies have to be fed and bathed and taken for rides in their buggies just the same as little girls. Isn't that what you wanted?"

"You p-promised me a baby sister and you — you *never* broke a promise to me, before," she sobbed.

"I'm sorry, dear. But after all, God does the deciding. We accept whichever He sends, just the way we accepted you, and love it just the same. Don't you see, darling?"

A horrible thought hit her. "M-maybe you wanted a boy! M-maybe you wanted a boy instead of me, even. Did you?" Without waiting for his reply, she went on, almost wildly now, "You love him already! You love him!"

"But of course I love him!"

"B-better than me?" she asked, between sobs.

"Come now, don't be absurd, Joanie. You're a big girl and you're working yourself up to — " He sounded almost annoyed; all the joy seemed to have gone from his voice.

"You do! I can tell! You love him best, because he's so little and because he's a boy. And I hate him! I don't ever want to see him!"

Her father's tenderness seemed to evaporate and he looked as though he had been slapped unexpectedly. He stood there and watched as she thumped her pillow and turned away from him to face the wall. Then he said in a stern voice, "I just can't believe all this, Joanie. How can you feel this way about an innocent, helpless little baby?" He shook his head slowly, then abruptly put out the light and left the room.

Alone, there in the dark, Joanie fixed her eyes upon the ceiling until the tiny flecks of silver in the sugary-textured plaster became visible. Then she sighed deeply. Just to think this was to have been the happiest day of her life! The day she had been looking forward to for such a long time. And the very worst part of it all was that Daddy was so pleased. So pleased, in fact, that he had forgotten to listen to her prayers. Oh well, she didn't feel like saying prayers tonight. She thumped her pillow again, yawned, and rolled over. Maybe she would wake up in the morning and discover that all this had been a dream, that the baby had still to arrive, that —

Joanie was fast asleep.

TWO

JOANIE AND HER FATHER avoided talking about the baby much during the next few days. It was as though each one knew the subject would be painful to the other. Then, on the morning before Mrs. Sanders was to come home from the hospital, Mr. Sanders announced, "Joanie, your mother thinks it would be nice for you to choose a name for the baby. I agree with her."

"Me? Why me? Don't mothers choose their babies' names? I mean, when I have a baby, I shall choose the name myself."

"Well, you did seem rather insistent upon Gwendolyn for this one, if I remember rightly," her father reminded her.

"I — I know. It was sweet of Mother to let me. But I think it was because she liked the name too. But there aren't any pretty names for a boy. I don't care what he's named. You and Mother choose a name for him."

"A boy wouldn't want a pretty name. He would want a name that sounded fine and that other boys liked. We thought perhaps you, knowing so many boys, would have a good idea as to what names are in favor these days."

17

"Daddy, I really don't care. Boys don't have popular names, just dreary ones like — like — " She spread jelly on her roll carefully and started to eat. Breakfast, with her father as cook, was a simple affair.

Impatiently, Mr. Sanders said, "Don't be ridiculous. Of course boys have their likes and dislikes. They happen to be human beings, no matter what else you think they are. And I think you would be hurting your mother's feelings after her being so generous as to let you choose, instead of just choosing a name herself." He reached for the salt and shook so much on his boiled egg that he most certainly was not aware of what he was doing.

Joanie grimaced at the sight and then asked, somewhat timidly, "Do you think he would blame me if he didn't like the name when he gets big?"

"We won't tell him you chose it until we discover how he feels about it. How's that?" Mr. Sanders suggested. Then he took a forkful of egg and made a face. "My goodness, this hen must have used a salt box for a nest," he declared.

For the first time in days, Joanie smiled. It might be fun, choosing a name, sharing a secret about it with Daddy. It suddenly became very important to her to find just the right name for the tiny, red-haired intruder who could do nothing but accept it, no matter what. It gave her a delightful sense of power over all boys everywhere. But because this was her own brother and part of the family, like it or not, the name must be something special. It must be a name she, at least, would always like.

All the way to school she thought about it. She

wondered what certain name in the whole wide world would suit a boy right from the time he was born to the time he became an old man like Grandfather. She knew a girl, for instance, whose parents always called her Toodles. Now wasn't that a predicament for the girl by the time she was grown up?

She tried out names, pronouncing them silently. My brother, James? No. How about Arthur? Like King Arthur of the Round Table. Arthur Sanders? Oh dear, no. That was Daddy's middle name, which would make the baby sort of Junior in a way, wouldn't it? Without the Roger that was Daddy's first name? She wasn't sure, but in any case she doubted the baby would like it later on. Roger was a nice enough name, but being her father's, she couldn't quite picture a baby in the family with the same name. Besides, no boy of her acquaintance appreciated being called Junior. They all wanted a name they could truly call their own. In this, at least, she agreed with the boys. Everyone had a right to his own name. Unless, of course, the father happened to have been Abraham Lincoln or George Washington.

She sighed. What if her brother should turn out to be President some day? Now there was a thought for you! But why should only boys have a chance to be President? No wonder they were so high and mighty when they knew no girl could ever — But why not? Was there a law saying a girl could never become President of the United States? She decided to find out. But back to the baby. President Roger Arthur Sanders! Junior? Or would The Second sound better? Silly either way. And here she was, a new baby brother without even a name, and already she was imagining him as President!

In school, she again earned a reprimand from Miss Perkins. "Joanie, come back from wherever you are!" the teacher said in a hopeless tone.

The class giggled and Joanie blushed. "Oh! Oh, I'm sorry, Miss Perkins. I — I was just thinking of names. I have to find one for my new brother."

"I see. Well, suppose you come to the board and see if you can solve this problem for us first. Afterwards perhaps we can help solve yours." Miss Perkins smiled and Joanie thought the teacher could be really very nice when she chose to be.

Joanie went to the board, solved the problem satisfactorily, and returned to her seat. But arriving there, she remembered something. She asked, "Miss Perkins, can a girl ever become President of the United States?"

There was a groan that went all through the class and some boy laughed derisively. Miss Perkins quieted the class at once.

"There is certainly no law preventing women from holding such a position," she answered.

"Only, the boys wouldn't vote for one," Joanie sighed, sitting down and setting her chin defiantly.

Then she heard Miss Perkins say, "Well, how about a name for the new baby? Shall we all make suggestions?"

The boys seemed pleased at the chance and soon quite a noisy debate was in progress. Miss Perkins again called for order and said, "Anyone with a suggestion should raise a hand and we will consider the name. Otherwise — "

Hands shot up and Susy Jones was given permission to speak.

"I like David," she said, timidly.

Joanie considered it. It was a fine name all right. Brave, for sure. Still, there were so many Davids, including David Wagner who sat near her and was always sneezing. Not David, she decided, avoiding David Wagner's hopeful glance.

"My favorite name for a boy is Hercules," Timmy Smith ventured, shyly. "Hercules was very strong, he even killed a huge snake with his own two hands when he was only six months old! You couldn't want a stronger boy than that!"

Timmy was not a strong boy. He was forever catching colds. He looked wistful as he spoke of Hercules.

"The snake was enormous, Miss Perkins, and it was just about to kill Hercules," he added, appealing directly to the teacher.

Joanie gave the name some thought. It was quite unusual and it was certainly impressive. But finally she said, "It's a good name, all right, but it does sound rather odd, I think. People might call him Herky or something like that and it wouldn't do at all, would it?"

"Peter? That's a strong name too," someone else suggested. "I learned in Sunday School that it means strong as a rock."

"Bruce? Randolph? Percy? Cedric?" The names were coming fast now and, one by one, were being discarded. Presently someone said, "How about Daniel? Daniel was brave and good and strong. And he had bushels of hair — "

"That was Samson," Joanie derided, but she found herself trying out this new suggestion with interest. "Well, there's that song we sing in Sunday School —

Dare To Be A Daniel. And I do like the name. Daniel fought lions and they are even worse than snakes. And he could be called Danny while he's little. Yes, I think Daniel is just about perfect!"

After that the class had to settle down to lessons again but Joanie felt happier than she had for several days. She could hardly wait to tell her father the name she had decided upon.

Mr. Sanders seemed very pleased with her choice. He said no one could wish for a finer name than Daniel and he was sure the baby would be satisfied with it when he grew old enough to care.

"Your mother will be so glad," he said. "She has to give the baby's name to the hospital before she brings him home, you know. I'm glad it's all settled. I think I'll telephone her this very minute and tell her about it — or better still, why don't you tell her? She would love to talk to you; she has missed you so much, Joanie."

After talking to her mother, Joanie could hardly wait until the following day to have her back home again. It was Friday and the afternoon session at school was short, due to a teachers' meeting. Joanie raced to the bus the moment the dismissal gong sounded. It seemed to take forever for the bus to load. But at long last she reached home and burst into the house as though she had been shot from a cannon.

"Mother! Oh, Mother! I'm home!" she called before she had the front door shut.

"In the living room, darling," came the gay, eager reply in her mother's voice.

At the living room door Joanie stopped short. Mother was sitting on the davenport and in front of her was a blue bassinette looking very much out of place. It seemed to take over the entire room. Joanie hardly noticed her mother's outstretched arms.

"Darling! Come here and let me look at you! I do believe you have grown two inches since I saw you last!" Mrs. Sanders exclaimed, beaming at Joanie. "Maybe you look so big because I have been looking at Danny for — "

Joanie, on her way to her mother's side, stopped again. Why did she have to spoil it by mentioning *him?* This was to have been a moment for just herself and her mother, kissing and hugging and telling one another how wonderful it was for Mother to be home again. But that bassinette stood there between them, and Joanie couldn't even get to her mother without either walking around it or leaning across it. She stood in mute dismay.

Mother hardly seemed to notice. "Come see him, Joanie! He's perfectly adorable! Would you like to hold him?"

Joanie just shook her head and walked slowly toward her mother to give her the kind of kiss one usually gives to a distant and slightly known relative. Still, Mrs. Sanders didn't seem to notice anything amiss.

"Look, he's awake," she said softly. "You can see his eyes — just as green as a pussy cat's! Come, little precious, let Joanie see you!" Mrs. Sanders leaned over the bassinette and took up a bundle of soft blue. Somehow, she managed to draw Joanie down beside her and, before Joanie knew it, the baby was on her own lap. He felt warm and he smelled like violets. Try as she would, she could not help looking down at the tiny, puckered red face. He yawned. Such an incredible sight!

"He's sleepy, I think," said Joanie. And then she couldn't see his face any longer because hot tears were filming her eyes.

Suddenly the baby was back in his bed and Joanie was in her mother's arms sobbing her heart out. It was both pain and pleasure to feel the warm embrace, to know that at last there was someone who could understand. "I — I m-missed you so, Mother! Don't ever go away again, will you?"

"I'll try not to, darling. I'm glad you missed me, though. We all like to be missed once in a while. I was beginning to think you and Daddy were getting along beautifully without me. But now here we are, all together, a perfect little family. I'm so happy, darling, aren't you?" Mrs. Sanders kissed Joanie gently on the forehead.

"If you could have brought a little girl instead — " Joanie faltered, almost inaudibly.

"Within a week you'll be wondering why on earth you ever wanted a little sister," her mother predicted with a smile of confidence. Joanie felt sorry for her.

Within a week? Surely Mother didn't really believe

that. Still, here in Mother's arms, she could feel no resentment toward her. And it probably wasn't Mother's fault God had thought she should have a little son. Mother was making the best of it, of course.

As the days and weeks went by, Joanie learned to hold the baby, to give him his bottle, and once in awhile she wheeled him up and down the street in his buggy. She did this, she kept reminding herself, because Danny was so helpless and it pleased Mother that she helped with him once in awhile.

The moment when Danny gave Joanie his very first real smile she almost forgot about his being a boy and bent over and kissed him. As she started to straighten up, his tiny fingers caught in her hair. She winced at the unexpected tug. "You're a boy, all right! Up to their tricks already!" she scolded, and glared at her mother for laughing.

THREE

ONE DAY DURING EARLY SUMMER, Mr. Sanders came home with some news. Mrs. Sanders was busy in the kitchen making hamburger patties and splitting rolls for a backyard barbecue supper. Joanie was setting the patio table and wishing Daddy would hurry home because she was hungry.

"Why do people always feel so much hungrier when there's something extra good for dinner, Mother?" she asked, taking knives and forks from a drawer in the kitchen. Her mother laughed but before she could answer, Mr. Sanders came in.

"Hah! Hamburgers! Hope there're plenty of them. I'm famished," he said jovially.

"That makes two of you," his wife answered as she set the patties aside and began slicing tomatoes. "The rest of it is up to you. Will you get the fire started, Roger? I'll feed Danny while you do it. By the way, what have you on your mind? You look mighty pleased about something!" Mrs. Sanders looked excited as she added, "Did you get it, Roger?"

"Get what?" Joanie asked.

"A quart of cherry vanilla ice cream," her father re-

26

plied with a grin she new well. It meant that he was teasing. Oh, he had brought home the ice cream all right, but there was something else, she knew.

"Don't tease," she said, pretending to pout.

"Roger, I'm dying to know," Mrs. Sanders put in.

"Impatient creatures! All right, I'll tell you, though I wanted to break the news while we ate. Yes, I got it!"

Mrs. Sanders laid down the slicing knife and threw her arms around her husband's neck. Joanie stood by in sheer bewilderment.

"Am I a part of this family or am I just a picture hanging on the wall?" she demanded.

"Oh, darling, I'd forgotten you didn't know about it." Mrs. Sanders sounded a bit contrite. "We didn't say anything before in case nothing came of it, but now everything seems to be settled. We're going to live in the mountains beside a lovely big lake! Daddy has a new school!"

"Oh." Joanie's lack of enthusiasm didn't seem to dampen her mother's spirits at all.

"That isn't all, Joanie. We wouldn't consider it were it not for the fact that Daddy will be the principal there. Aren't you proud?"

"Principal? Oh, Daddy, how wonderful!" Turning to her mother, Joanie went on, "I bet he'll be the best principal in the whole world!"

"Well, thank you, sweetie-pie. That's the nicest compliment a father could expect to receive from a daughter. But that fire isn't going to get started all by itself — " He hurried off to get the charcoal and starter fluid, and Joanie began wondering what it was going to be like living by a lake in the mountains.

Each summer the family spent two weeks at Lake Chippewa where they lived in a small cabin with a tiny kitchen and only one bedroom. There was a davenport in the living room that made into a bed for Joanie at night. And after she was supposed to be asleep she would still be listening to all the unfamiliar country noises outside — frogs and crickets and owls and goodness only knew what else. Not that she was scared, but anyone who said it was quiet in the country couldn't have spent much time there. It was a lot easier to sleep to the sound of automobile horns and other city noises, she had complained once. But Mother had said that was only because she was used to the city.

"Won't we ever live in this house again, Mother?" Joanie asked, somewhat dismayed. This was the only home she knew. She had lived here all her life.

"I'm afraid not," Mrs. Sanders answered.

"Won't you hate to give up the petunias and the pink rose bush? And what about my swing in the back yard?"

These and other thoughts came to disturb Joanie. She felt almost the way Alice must have right after hitting the bottom of the well during her adventures in Wonderland. Everything, but *everything*, would be different. Even her playmates and her school! "Mother, do you really want to go?" Joanie's face expressed her apprehension.

"Of course. And so does Daddy," her mother answered. "We can certainly grow more petunias and get another rose bush. We can take your swing with us. I think it will be great fun finding a new house and fixing it up just the way we want to. Remember those pretty pink ruffly curtains you liked so well at Mary Beth's house when we visited her? We could try to find some just like them for your room."

"Really? And a pink bedspread to match, maybe?"

"Yes, I believe we could manage that, too. Now, will you carry out the hamburgers so Daddy can get going?" Mrs. Sanders handed the meat platter to Joanie, who carried it out to her father very carefully.

"Daddy," she asked, while she watched him cook the hamburgers. "Won't you miss the old school? I mean, where everyone knows you?"

"That I will," he declared. "And the scent of the orange groves around here. It will take some getting used to, looking at Christmas trees instead of bridal blossoms!"

"Did you say Christmas trees?" Joanie looked puzzled.

"Yes, indeed," Mr. Sanders continued. "We won't have any trouble getting just the right one this year. And snow — you have never seen snow, have you, Joanie? What a treat you have in store! We'll get you a sled and you'll need boots — "

"Daddy, we aren't going to Alaska, are we?" Joanie interrupted, a little twinkle lighting her eyes.

"No," her father laughed, "not even outside California, for that matter. But we're going high. *So* high we'll be looking down into the clouds sometimes. And the sky up there is the bluest blue you ever set eyes on. Briarcliff Lake is a year-round resort, you know, with fishing and boating and all that in the summer, and skiing in the winter. How does that sound?"

"Can you ski, Daddy?" Joanie's interest was increasing.

"I could, at one time. And I understand they teach it to the youngsters in school up there. Part of the physical education program. That's living, Joanie!" He rubbed his hands together gleefully. It was impossible not to feel some of his enthusiasm. Maybe it *was* going to be fun. Maybe it was the loveliest place on earth. Only it was going to take a while getting used to it; of that Joanie was sure. But it would be wonderful being the daughter of the high school principal instead of the child of an English teacher who coached the football team and assisted the principal without ever having an office of his own. Golly, maybe Daddy might become President, some day! Why just waste time hoping it would be Danny who achieved such an honor? She giggled, and her father glanced at her inquiringly.

"I suppose now, instead of Mother always saying 'Go speak to your father about it —' she will say, 'Go to the Principal!' Golly!"

"So you'd just better start minding your *p*'s and *q*'s, young lady," her father laughed.

"How about my ABC's?" she pursued.

"And the dots on your *i*'s and the crosses on your *t*'s."

Joanie sighed. Then she said, without too much concern, "It sounds as if you aren't going to be too much fun to live with."

"Well, the burgers are ready. Call your mother, will you?" Mr. Sanders slipped the cooked patties expertly onto buns.

At last the three were seated around the umbrella-covered table, enjoying to the utmost the sizzling fare.

30

Danny sucked his thumb contentedly while Mother worried a little that perhaps he hadn't had enough to eat.

"Thumbs can be delicious at six months old, didn't you know?" Mr. Sanders said. "The nicest dessert a fellow could ask for."

"He'll have teeth like a gopher's," predicted Mrs. Sanders with a rueful little laugh. She gazed fondly upon her son, lying in his buggy nearby.

"Daddy, tell us more about the new place, will you?" begged Joanie. "How about *my* school? Is it far from where we will be living?"

"Since we don't yet know just where we will be living, that question cannot be answered," replied her father. "However, there is a house right on the lake front which I am hoping to get for us. If I do, your school will be a short bus ride away."

"You'll be terribly important, won't you, Daddy?"

Mr. Sanders suddenly became more serious.

"Joanie, the high school is very small. I've had as many students in one class here as there are in the entire high school at Briarcliff Lake. Why, the year-round population there is no bigger than five thousand and that includes parents and babies, grandparents and everyone else. The school is more appealing to me just because of this fact. I like having the personal contact with all the students and their parents which a small community affords. Of course my job will be important, but it isn't a job for a man who considers *himself* so important. There will be no cause for any member of this family to walk around with an up-tilted nose!"

He paused to give Joanie time to consider this and

31

then went on, "As for your school. It is even smaller than the high school. You can expect small classes and a great deal of individual attention, so you ought to be able to pull up your grades considerably."

"Oh." Joanie wished her father wouldn't always keep reminding her of her grades. She knew only too well what they were like. But then, being a teacher himself, she guessed he just couldn't help it.

"You'll love the place, darling, believe me. It's a paradise — wild life — "

Joanie almost choked on a swallow of lemonade as she exclaimed, "Wild life! Lions and tigers and — and grizzly bears?"

Mr. Sanders laughed. "Well, not quite. As I said before, we aren't leaving California, and while a mountain lion has been sighted at Briarcliff Lake on occasion, it isn't the general rule. Nor do such creatures prowl about our forests in herds. No, I was thinking of deer, squirrels, rabbits, chipmunks, and — yes, a bear or two, though I believe they prefer keeping out of sight most of the time. There are also all kinds of lovely birds in the summertime. I tell you — " Mr. Sanders was beginning to sound like an enthusiastic real estate salesman.

"And perfectly adorable mosquitos," put in Mrs. Sanders, realistically.

"But bears! Daddy, what if one should chase me up a tree?" Joanie turned wide blue eyes upon her father and feigned a delicious fright.

"Then, honey, you just wait up there till I come for you!"

"Honey is right," laughed Mrs. Sanders. "I do believe that is what they trap bears with. Or is that just a tale?"

"A bear's tail," her husband quipped back, to Joanie's great amusement.

Joanie helped herself to another hamburger — almost cold at this point — and spread it generously with ketchup and relish, chopped onion, and a thick slice of tomato. She placed the upper part of the bun on top of everything and then, attempting a giant bite, found her mouth too small to manage it. She removed the slice of tomato reluctantly, sneaking a glance at her parents as she did so. They were pretending not to have noticed. Before attempting another bite, she said, "I do hope my school is nice."

"The building is very attractive and almost new." Mr. Sanders seemed delighted to talk about Briarcliff Lake. "I met the teacher you will have and she seemed extraordinarily pleased to be getting a new girl — "

"Naturally," came Joanie's smug reply, "teachers don't like boys, either."

"Really? I always found them tolerable," her father said.

"Because you happen to have been one yourself," Joanie retorted, with a twisted little smile.

"The elementary school principal is a woman, by the way," Mr. Sanders continued.

This sounded interesting. Evidently girls counted for something at Briarcliff Lake. Joanie began looking forward to the move with increasing interest.

Joanie wondered how they would take her news at her present school, when she told her class about it. It was most gratifying, therefore, when Monday morning came and she announced that she would not be return-

ing for the fall semester, to hear them say, one by one,

"Oh Joanie, no!"

"Oh, what a shame, we shall miss you." This from Miss Perkins, who also added, "but of course it will be lovely for you — "

"Golly! But you'll be down for visits, won't you?"

Even the boys were fairly nice about it, Joanie thought. Not that they said much, but they didn't say anything mean either, which was significant!

And so she lived in a state of pleasant anticipation until, at long last, the move to Briarcliff Lake became a reality.

Mr. Sanders had managed to get the house he had spoken of and was pleased when his wife and daughter agreed with him that it was charming.

"Which is my room?" Joanie wanted to know, almost immediately upon arriving.

"The one at the top of the stairs — it overlooks the lake, dear. I think you will like it," her mother told her.

Like it? She loved it! From its large windows one could see all the activity on the water below — sailboats, rowboats, motorboats, canoes, fishermen, swimmers — all promised an entire world of what appeared to be wonderful fun. Just under Joanie's window was the small dock belonging to the house and she ran downstairs and outdoors in order to examine the small boat tied there.

"Daddy! A boat of our very own? Oh, I love you!"

"I love you, too," Mr. Sanders replied, grinning. "It needs a name — "

"May I choose it?"

"You seem to be good at name-choosing."

"What else but the *Jolly Roger?*" That was a happy inspiration, Joanie thought, seeing the pleased smile that spread over her father's face.

"H'm, I believe she really does love me!" he commented, watching her tear off towards the dock.

Joanie was wondering how soon she would be allowed to take the boat out alone when she heard a voice behind her, coming from the shore.

"Are you the new girl?"

Joanie turned at once and saw a girl of her own age, with the yellowest hair and the pinkest face she had ever encountered. She could not help but stare.

The girl was apparently used to this for she laughed and said, "I know. They call me Haystack around here. I don't really mind because — well — there's only one Haystack and there are seven Kathies."

Her eyes were twinkling merrily and Joanie liked her at once. Anyone who didn't mind a rather pointed nickname was a "good egg," so far as Joanie was concerned.

"What's your real name, though?" Joanie wanted to know.

"Oh — it doesn't really matter, does it, since everyone calls me — "

"Haystack? Well no, I suppose not, but — well, my name's Joanie. Joanie Sanders. Actually, it's just Joan, of course."

"Oh, all right. I'm Kathie Martin. Katherine, if you want it that way," the girl confessed, and Joanie suddenly realized that the girl actually liked her nickname.

It was probably something like the way she felt

36

when her father called her some absurd name like Muddlehead in an affectionate sort of way.

"We just came today," Joanie told Haystack. "My father's going to be the new principal at the high school." There was the slightest touch of pride in her voice.

"Oh yes, I know," Haystack said. "Everyone knows, of course. This is such a little place, really, after the summer people leave. When a year-round house gets rented, everyone wants to know who has taken it. My father operates the ski lift in the wintertime and the swimming pool during the summer."

"Lucky for you!" Joanie commented enviously.

"Is your father very strict with you?" Haystack asked.

"Not really. Why?" Joanie replied.

"I mean, principals won't stand for any goofing off, will they? But then maybe it's different with their own children. Say — maybe you'd better tell him the kids around here won't like it if you get special privileges." Haystack looked concerned.

Joanie laughed. "Golly, he won't be my principal for simply ages! I'll be going into Fourth, not Tenth, when school opens, you know!"

"Fourth? Miss Coles' room?" Haystack seemed unduly upset.

"Well, I don't know my teacher's name yet. But if she teaches Fourth, why I guess that's her — she — who she'll be."

"I guess your father's strict about your grammar," Haystack commented rather dolefully.

"Look, what did you mean about Miss Coles? Is

she awful, or something? Daddy said — " Joanie paused, a vague uneasiness stealing over her.

"Oh, Miss Coles is all right. Quite nice, as a matter of fact. It's only that — well — maybe I'd just better skip it. Or maybe you wouldn't care anyway. But I certainly don't want to be the one to — " Haystack's pink face grew pinker as she fumbled through and finally stopped talking. But after a short silence, she asked, "Do you like boys, Joanie?"

"I despise and loathe and hate them. Period." Joanie answered vehemently.

"You don't like them?" Haystack looked more upset than ever. Whatever was wrong with the girl?

"Haystack, you didn't answer me about Miss Coles. Is she — well — you make it sound as if she had two heads or something! What *is* it, anyway?"

"Oh — nothing. Honestly. She's really very nice."

It was quite evident that Haystack had said all she intended to say. During the ensuing silence, Joanie scuffed the toes of her sturdy moccasins in the gravel, her eyes cast down. Then her mother called her and Haystack said she guessed she'd better be going home.

"Tomorrow I'll take you around, if you like, to meet some of the kids," she called back as she hurried off.

FOUR

THE FOLLOWING DAY WAS Saturday and Haystack kept her promise. What left Joanie somewhat surprised was the discovery that none of the girls she met that day would be in her class. In each instance it was either Third grade or Fifth they would be entering on Monday morning. Still, Joanie thought, they weren't any of them too young or too old for her to play with. And on Monday, of course, she would meet those in her own grade. Altogether, there would be more girls than she had expected, she thought. Girls galore, in fact, from which to choose a special few for good friends.

In the meantime, she was shown all around by her new friend Haystack. Everywhere they went she was received with warmth and an obvious eagerness to make her feel welcome, so that when Monday morning arrived she didn't feel nearly so much the stranger she had expected to feel.

Haystack called for her, as she lived just a little farther along the shore road. It being Joanie's first day, however, her father was going with her. The high school did not start classes for two more days, which left Mr. Sanders free to accompany Joanie without interfering with his own schedule.

As Mrs. Sanders offered the girls an orange each, to eat during recess, she said to Joanie, "I know you are going to like your new school, Joanie. 'Bye, dear — "

Joanie, filled with confidence, kissed her mother and hurried off to her father's car. A saucy gray squirrel scampered up a tree as she passed by. The air was heady with the scent of pine trees. Oh, it really was lovely here, she thought. Already it smelled like Christmas!

But by the time school was dismissed — early because this was the first day — Joanie's heart had sunk to her shoes. Not the bright sunshine, the incredibly blue sky, the ever-present squirrels, or the tall, majestic pine trees could cheer her one iota. The song of a bird caused her to mutter to herself, "Oh, I wish I was a bird — a sparrow or a robin, or anything else except me." Life was so uncomplicated for birds. Or so it seemed to her just then. She boarded the bus, almost unaware of Haystack calling to her to wait, until the girl caught up with her. When she did notice her friend, Joanie said, "You knew, didn't you? Why on earth didn't you tell me, Haystack? Instead of — "

Haystack interrupted. "Joanie, I'm awfully sorry — but it wouldn't have helped any, my telling you, would it? I mean, it would just have ruined your week end."

"Anyone who wants to be my friend had just better be honest," Joanie replied sulkily, turning her face toward the window of the bus as she took a seat next to it. She ignored Haystack on the ride home, knowing all the time that it wasn't the other girl's fault. But it seemed

40

to help, at a time like this, to hurt someone. By tomorrow, perhaps, she would be ready to tell Haystack that she was sorry, but for now —

She ran all the way from the bus stop to her house. Once she had told Mother of the awful fate that had befallen her, Joanie knew something would be done about it. Mothers always took care of everything! Out of breath, she burst into the house, found her mother preparing lunch, and flung herself upon her. "Mother! Oh, Mother, I'm going to die! Absolutely die!"

"Darling, please! Please just let me set the baked beans down. If you're going to die anyway, there isn't much point in getting all burned and scalded first by a pot of beans, is there?" said Mrs. Sanders, focusing her attention on the beans.

"But I mean it, Mother! You've got to be serious! I'll really die if you don't do something quick. You just won't believe it!"

"Try me and see," Mrs. Sanders suggested, setting the beans down on the table. Then, taking Joanie by the shoulders, she continued, "But first sit down and calm yourself. You can tell me just as well sitting down across the table from me as half-strangling me, wouldn't you say? Please let go my — "

Joanie did as she was told and sat down, while her mother began to serve the food. There were little cut-up frankfurters in the beans, a dish Joanie had always considered her favorite luncheon dish. But today she didn't feel hungry and she began at once, "It's perfectly awful! I just can't stay here, Mother! I won't stay in that awful school!"

"Awful?" Mrs. Sanders frowned. "Daddy said — "

"Absolutely hideous."

"All right, let's get down to facts. I have no idea what you are talking about, you know. Why not eat something first? Maybe you are hungry — you ate very little breakfast, you were too excited — "

"Little did I know! I'm not *hungry*, Mother!"

It took only another glance in her mother's direction, however, for Joanie to realize she had better get on with the matter before her mother's patience ran out.

"Boys!" she said, taking up her fork. "Nothing but boys! I'm *the only girl*, Mother! Nine boys and *me*, in Fourth! Mother, please, what can we do?" Tears were starting to her eyes now the story was told, and it was gratifying to see signs of dismay in her mother's face.

Mrs. Sanders put down the big serving spoon and frowned. "Oh, dear," she said, "this really is an unusual situation, isn't it? My goodness!"

"Unusual? Is that all you can say, Mother? It's

absolutely awful, a fate worse than death! I mean, I'd rather be dead than — than be the only girl!"

"Darling, I admit it may be somewhat disconcerting to you, and of course we can see what we can do. Not that I share your revulsion for little boys, mind you, but the situation does call for — well — suppose we just wait for Daddy to come in and let him share the problem? I'm sure he will think of something, dear. Now, do eat your lunch. I fixed the beans especially for you."

Mechanically, Joanie took a forkful of food. Then she said, somewhat more calmly, "The thing is, they don't want me any more than I want to be there. I know, because I heard them talking at recess. One boy said to another, 'What does a stupid old girl want, coming to our room to spoil everything?' As if he really thought I'd planned it that way!"

"How about the teacher?"

"Miss Coles? She said, 'Well, at last we have a girl in our class. Boys, this is Joanie Sanders. I'm sure you will all make her feel welcome among us.' And then she told me to sit at the end of the second row next to a real mean-looking boy. He pretended he didn't see me. He looks like Dracula — " With that, Joanie made a face that caused her mother to laugh.

Just then, Danny awakened from his midday nap. He announced the fact with a loud wail, bringing his mother on the run.

Joanie muttered, resentfully, "Oh, be quiet, you — you *boy*, you!" She took up her fork again and this time finished her lunch.

Joanie's problem was presented to her father at dinner that evening. He was hardly reassuring. In fact, by the time he had said his final piece, Joanie was almost wishing she had never told him and had left it to her mother to handle.

"If that's the situation, Joanie, I doubt there is much we can do about it. Sooner or later other girls are bound to join you, I'm sure," he said.

"You can't mean we are just going to forget the whole thing, Daddy?" Joanie cried in disbelief.

"Well, have you any suggestions?" he asked reasonably.

"C-couldn't you go talk to the principal or something?" Joanie fixed appealing eyes upon him.

Mrs. Sanders put in, "You could do that much, Roger."

"But can the principal cause nine little boys to disappear? What would their parents say?" Mr. Sanders' attempt at humor was lost on both Joanie and her mother.

"Still, she might have an idea," Mrs. Sanders persisted, her sympathetic eyes on Joanie.

"Well, we'll try," Mr. Sanders finally agreed, sounding pessimistic. He added gravely, "Sometimes situations arise which we can't help, you know. And sometimes it's a good idea, if you can't change the situation, to change your attitude toward it."

"Humph!" Joanie all but snorted. Then she said, "I'm sorry — I didn't mean to be rude. B-but it's easy to — "

"I know. But Joanie, I don't want you thinking I can accomplish the impossible. I said I would try," Mr. Sanders said, a little more kindly.

So long as he tried! Joanie was confident he could

do something if only he tried. However, just in case he failed, Joanie decided to prepare for the worst. Since it was absurd to think they could move away from here, she must armor herself.

"I shall wear my hair tied very high up so the boys can't tie it to the desk behind me," she declared. "And I shall never wear a dress with a full skirt. On windy days boys always laugh and tease you when your dress blows up. And I shall wear my sneakers all the time, too, because sometimes leather shoes squeak. I certainly wouldn't want the boys to waste their precious time thinking I was trying to attract their attention in *any* way. I would actually like to cut my hair very short and wear blue jeans, but then they'd surely think I wanted to be a boy. They are too stupid to realize I would be going to school like that just so they would leave me alone. Oh, if they'd only all get lost!" Tears threatened again and she clenched her fists angrily.

Far from showing further sympathy, Mr. Sanders suddenly lost patience. He said, "For goodness' sake, Joanie, what makes you think you matter to them one way or the other? I am sure they will have many other things to attract their attention in spite of your presence among them."

"Oh, you don't know," Joanie almost shouted. "You simply don't know, if you can talk like that! Why, boys get more fun out of making a girl look silly than anything! Just try telling a joke to them — they pretend they don't get it and ask you to please let them know when it's time to laugh!"

"I think you're obsessed," Mr. Sanders continued, and Joanie frowned over the unfamiliar word. She refused to ask its meaning but she was sure it was not complimentary. Her father went on, "May I make a suggestion? Instead of making yourself as disagreeable as possible, why not try being the nicest girl they have ever met? Look pretty, be polite, share things with them — be, in fact, totally disarming. Disarming, in case you don't know, means — "

"I never heard anything so silly," Joanie interrupted.

"Be that as it may, you might as well face the fact that boys are here to stay, and we really need them, your opinion to the contrary. Has it ever occurred to you that fathers began life as little boys? Wouldn't it be a strange world if there were no fathers? Who, may I ask, would pay for new shoes and bicycles?"

Joanie ate the rest of her dinner in silence. Daddy just didn't understand. How could he, having been a boy himself?

As Mr. Sanders had predicted, nothing much could be done about Joanie's predicament. Mrs. Westcott, the principal, was sympathetic and understanding enough. She even went so far as to make a suggestion, but it proved impractical, as she herself admitted. It was that Joanie should be placed in a different grade.

At first, Joanie was heartened by the suggestion, but she soon realized it couldn't work. A different grade simply meant that she would have to be demoted to Third. Joanie could not, Mrs. Westcott explained, be skipped a class since her grades from the previous year did not merit such procedure. Also, it was no longer considered in the best interests of pupils to have them skip grades.

"You would be bound to miss something, no matter how industrious you were," the principal said with a kindly smile. "Still, under the circumstances — "

"I know," Joanie agreed, realizing at once that to skip a grade would mean a tremendous amount of studying. On the other hand, to go backward would be unthinkable. "I'd never go back to Third," she stated vehemently.

"Nor would I permit it," her father decided gravely. To Mrs. Westcott, he said, "Joanie has the ability to do better work. It is simply a lack of concentration on her part. I feel she could definitely do fifth-grade work if she really applied herself. But she has to have the inclination toward it first, of course. At this point, I wouldn't want her to try. She ought first to prove herself willing, don't you think, Mrs. Westcott?"

"Yes indeed," the principal answered. "There is one other possibility in that regard. If Joanie would try very hard during the first semester and come up with some exceptionally good grades, we could then consider a mid-term promotion for her."

Discouraged, Joanie could only say, "It would be better than returning to Third, I guess."

"Good girl." Her father patted her on the shoulder approvingly. "Really, darling, it won't be so bad. Boys aren't really monsters. They — "

"They only seem so, most of the time," Joanie observed with a derisive little smile.

Mr. Sanders took his leave and Joanie went to her classroom. She was suddenly determined to work so hard that by the end of January there would be no question as to her fitness to enter Fifth. There she would take her place along with Haystack and Laura and Christie, three of the girls she had come to know. While they were slightly older than she, she felt on a par with them and knew they would be pleased to have her in their class.

In Fifth, there were presently six boys and five girls. An even dozen, once she joined them, and perfectly matched. In the meantime, she meant to take Haystack's suggestion to join the Brownies and thus spend at least a few hours each week with no one but girls in the group.

Because she worked so hard during social studies and spelling that afternoon, the time seemed to fly. After that came recess and a reunion with Haystack, to tell her and the other girls what the plans were.

Back in class again, it was time for physical ed. There was a lot of noisy shuffling while the children filed back onto the playground where they were to play ball. "Just 'catch,'" Miss Coles said amiably as she threw the first ball to a boy named James. He caught it and immediately threw it toward a boy they called Jackie, watching the latter pass it swiftly to the boy wearing thick-lensed glasses.

"Take off your glasses, Archie," Miss Coles said quickly.

Archie missed the ball as he started to obey the teacher. But then he objected, above the noise of the game, "If I take them off, Miss Coles, I can't see to catch."

"Oh, all right, but do be careful. Go ahead, throw the ball — "

The ball passed from boy to boy and soon there was only Joanie who hadn't had a turn. She was feeling quite miserable when, suddenly, the teacher herself caught the ball and threw it to Joanie. Taken unawares, Joanie missed and a chorus of groans went up.

The boys' comments included: "Aw, what a fumble!" "What can you expect from a girl, anyway?" "Wouldn't you know it!"

Joanie heard them all and felt her face redden. Impulsively, she snatched up the ball at her feet and threw it wildly in the last speaker's direction. To her surprise, he caught it, grinned, and threw it hard and fast toward someone else. It came back to Joanie just as swiftly and, once again, unexpectedly.

Mortified by this second failure, she suffered such insults as, "Oh, for Pete's sake, get lost!" "Boy, what a stupe!" "Butterfingers! Get a net!"

Miss Coles called to her, "Throw it, Joanie. Don't listen to them!"

With all her strength, Joanie hurled the ball. The boy at whom the ball was aimed failed to catch it. But instead of being embarrassed, as she had expected, he cried out contemptuously, "Spaghetti arm! Can't even throw — !" Joanie looked at Miss Coles helplessly.

"Don't let them upset you, Joanie," the teacher said. "They yell at one another like that all the time. The worst thing you can do is let them think it bothers you. If you do, you'll really be in for it! Just pretend you think they're funny and you'll have no trouble — "

Joanie felt somewhat encouraged by the fact that Miss Coles seemed to understand and, for the rest of the game, she did much better.

During the afternoon Miss Coles announced that they would have a reading test to discover how advanced the class was. Each pupil would read aloud from one of the new books. Joanie felt herself on safe ground here. She loved to read aloud and to be read to. She opened her copy with confidence. She saw that the book had some very nice illustrations along with the text.

The story about to be read concerned the American flag and Betsy Ross's part in designing it. When Joanie's turn came, she read with all the fervor and expression she could muster. No longer was she a lone little girl standing in a classroom filled with boys. She was Betsy Ross and the flag was the most important thing in the world. She became so carried away that she was unaware of the snickering going on behind her until Miss Coles clapped her hands together loudly in a command for silence.

"Boys! Boys!"

Joanie stopped reading. She heard a boy nearby whisper to the boy she knew as Bobby, "Who does she think she is — a movie star?"

"Yeah. Boy!" Bobby scoffed.

"Tommy Mason, if you have any comments, kindly address them to the entire class . . . Joanie, that was splendid. You read beautifully." Miss Coles gave Joanie a reassuring smile. Then she turned a severe face to the boys. "Some of you would do well to take a cue from Joanie and put a little expression into your reading, which would indicate that you understand what you read. And also care, incidentally. All right, Tommy. You may show us how well you can read; take it from where Joanie left off, please."

Tommy didn't know where Joanie had left off. He turned a page or two in a flustered manner, stammered excuses, and then, inspired, coughed hard. "I — I guess I have a cold," he muttered unhappily.

"You seemed to be perfectly well before recess," came Miss Coles' rather withering comment before she called upon someone else to read.

Joanie's respect for Miss Coles increased. She guessed no boy really fooled *her!* By the end of the day, Joanie was in a much more cheerful state of mind. She felt she could count on the teacher in a crisis. Of course, this was only the second day at school so perhaps it was too early to tell.

FIVE

As the weeks went by, Joanie became better acquainted with her classmates. Some, she admitted, were not so bad. Not that she actually liked any of the boys, but there were times when she was a bit surprised by what she termed their behavior toward her. As, for instance, the time she dropped her arithmetic book and Archie Polster picked it up for her as casually as if it had been his own book.

Her father asked her one evening, "Well, Joanie, how are you getting along with the boys?"

"Must we talk about it?" she asked with a slight shrug.

"I think so. Your mother and I happen to be interested in something you made such a big to-do over not so long ago," he replied. He began to open his newspaper with an impatient gesture.

Joanie was familiar with this gesture of her father's. It meant he was slightly annoyed and expected a respectful answer.

She said, "Well, you know how boys are — "

Mr. Sanders laid down his newspaper and said, "I remember how they were when I was one. They were tolerable."

"Sure. In the olden days they behaved themselves. But they are absolute monsters these days." Joanie seemed very sure of herself and her assertion.

Mrs. Sanders laughed and shot a teasing glance in her husband's direction. Then she said, "Don't you believe it, Joanie. I knew your father when he was a boy — we went to school together, you know — "

"I'd forgotten your telling me that. But Mother, Daddy couldn't have been such a dog! You would never have married him — " Joanie looked incredulous and her mother laughed again.

"Darling, he was a beast! But, of course, I waited for him to grow up before I married him. I must say at the time he was your age, I never — "

Mrs. Sanders was interrupted by her husband. "If you dare go into details, Margaret, I'll tell about the time you threw the egg at me — !"

"Roger, that isn't fair! You know very well I thought it was one of the hard-boiled ones!" Mrs. Sanders' protest was merry, her eyes twinkling at the memory.

"You mean you threw an egg in Daddy's face?" Joanie was enjoying this. She gave her mother her most respectful attention, then giggled.

"Indeed she did. Not only that, it was uncooked and, by the odor, was at least five years old. If I sniff hard enough, I can still smell it! Ugh!" Mr. Sanders grimaced.

Mrs. Sanders went on to explain. "It was a contest, Joanie. Someone — a boy, undoubtedly — slipped the uncooked egg in among the hard-boiled ones and I was the one unlucky enough to — "

"*You* were unlucky! Come now, it was *my* face!" Mr. Sanders grinned. He turned to his daughter. "Getting back to the monsters in Fourth, however. How about them, Joanie?"

"Well, to begin with," Joanie answered, "there's Archie. He's rather a pill, but I think he likes me. Eric is — oh, *square*. He sort of likes me too, though. But Tommy! Speaking of monsters! There's James — he makes everyone sick, honestly. Even the boys."

Mr. Sanders crossed his legs and leaned back in his chair, looking pensive. "A pill, a monster and a square," he recited, his eyes upon the ceiling. "Aren't there any human beings in the class? Tell us — what makes Archie a pill? And Tommy a monster? And Eric a square?" Mr. Sanders turned to his wife and began to explain what a square was. "A square was once an — " He shrugged as Mrs. Sanders indicated she already understood.

Joanie said, "Archie is all right, I suppose. Only he competes all the time. You know the type, Daddy. I mean, if I happen to get ninety in arithmetic, Archie simply has to get ninety-one. His father's a professor, you know."

"I see," said Mr. Sanders. "Archie must be Doctor Polster's boy. Polster is here on sabbatical leave, writing a book, I believe." This latter information was addressed to Mrs. Sanders, who appeared properly impressed.

Joanie looked perplexed. "What's a sabba — sabbat — ?" She stumbled over the unfamiliar word which sounded intriguing.

"It's a vacation given to college and university professors every seven years," her father explained. "They may use the time to rest, but it is usually hoped they will spend the period in study or writing books, or in travel."

"Imagine studying when you don't have to!" Joanie murmured.

"H'm . . . Well, to get back to our young — er — friends, the monster and his pals."

"Well, naturally, Eric isn't a monster," Joanie told him.

"Why naturally?" her father asked.

Joanie smiled. "Well, when your father's a minister! The kids say Eric isn't allowed to do anything that's fun. I think it's weird."

"Darling, you're exaggerating," her mother chided. "And even if you aren't, how does it affect you?"

"Well, he isn't like any other boy, that's how."

"Ah, he has you stumped!" Mr. Sanders sounded amused.

Joanie chose to ignore the remark and went on, "He opens doors for teachers and is very polite and never gets into fights or anything like other boys do. It's weird, that's all. I can't stand perfect people, they bore me."

"I should think you would find it most refreshing to have a boy in your class who doesn't run with the pack," Mr. Sanders commented. He turned back to his paper.

"He sounds like a little gentleman to me," Mrs. Sanders remarked to Joanie as she took up some knitting from the table nearby.

"Oh, he's that, all right. He seems to like me, but golly, Mother, he's even nicer than I am!"

Her words brought both parents up with a start. Her father said, "Well! Of all the conceit!" He sounded stupefied. Her mother remained silent, looking dumb-

founded.

Joanie was undisturbed. She giggled and said, "Oh, don't look like that. I don't mean I'm really nice, I just mean people think I am. I mean, I always watch my manners and I don't yell in public — much — and, well, I'm a girl!"

"Bully for you," was her father's inelegant comment as he scratched the top of his head in wonderment. He became thoughtful for a moment or two. Presently he said, "Joanie, I'd like to tell you a little story. It has a moral and I know such stories bore you. But let's risk it. I've a feeling you will like it anyway."

Resignedly, Joanie said, "I don't really mind a moral if the story is fun. Go ahead, Daddy."

"Well, once upon a time there lived a Bedouin. That is to say, an Arab who lived in the barren desert in the most primitive manner. He had a very stupid wife named Farida, who considered herself very beautiful. It is hard to tell how she came to this conclusion since she had never owned a mirror and her only reflection came from a bucketful of water drawn from the well.

"Anyway, the Arab was quite contented with her. A man needed a wife to cook and sew and wash for him, all of which Farida did well enough. To show his appreciation of her, he would bring her some little trinket from the village whenever he made one of his rare trips there.

"One day, he found it necessary to go to the village. He would be away, as usual, for several days, since travel by camel is no speedy method. He promised to bring a present back to Farida and she awaited his return eagerly.

"But when Abdullah returned, there was no present. Farida was ready to sulk until he explained, 'I wanted to bring you something very splendid, my dear wife, but it cost too much and I will have to wait until I have enough to pay for it. I promise you that you will have your gift for the *Ramadan Feast.*'

"So Farida waited through two more of Abdullah's journeys, but still there was no gift. Her patience was wearing thin. She found it very difficult to keep quiet about it, but custom forbade an Arab wife to criticize her husband, so she remained silent.

"Then, a few days after his return from his most recent trip, his wife started to clean his tent. She lifted a rug to shake it out and underneath it, in a far corner, she found a flat package. She lifted it, finding it rather heavy for its size. Curiosity got the best of her and she removed the wrappings. There was nothing but a square object that would not bend, painted grey all over.

" 'Now why would Abdullah want to hide a thing like this? And whatever can it be?' she muttered.

"Then, still reluctant to replace it, she turned the object over. Suddenly she exclaimed in amazement. A face stared up at her — the face of a woman, leathery of skin, sullen and stupid looking. The more Farida stared into the mirror — for that of course is what it was — the more the reflection changed. The woman staring back at her looked angry, her eyes grew sharper, her nose pinched. Altogether, she was certainly just about the ugliest creature one could imagine. Whoever this awful looking woman was, thought Farida, she could not look at her miserable face any longer. She flung the mirror across the tent. It hit against a large crockery urn standing by the entrance and shattered to bits. Now for the first time in many a week, Farida smiled contentedly.

"Just then, Abdullah entered the tent. Seeing what his wife had done, he cried out, 'Farida! What is this thing you have done? Your gift — why have you broken it? Five sheep in all it cost me, and I carried it so carefully all the miles back from the village! The most wonderful gift in the world, to the most beautiful wife in the world!'

"Farida turned on him angrily and cried, 'You find for yourself another wife in the village! You bring me a likeness of her, painted on glass, and expect me to be grateful! How, pray tell, could you find a woman of such ugliness of face? Bah!'

"Sadly, Abdullah surveyed the broken mirror and looked in misery upon his wife. Then he said very quietly, 'Did you not know that beauty is in the eye of the beholder? For the first time, I see you as you really are — ' " Mr. Sanders concluded his story and contemplated his daughter.

Joanie remained deep in thought for several moments. Then, with a smile of understanding, she said, "I see what it means, Daddy. You can see what you want to see in anyone — "

"Something like that," Mr. Sanders said quietly.

"Daddy, do you suppose the Arab went on loving his wife just the same?"

"Possibly. But I doubt he would ever find her as beautiful again. So just keep the story in mind whenever you begin to feel too satisfied with yourself. That was the point I was trying to make, really." He pinched her cheek fondly and went on, "Now, how about Tommy-the-Monster and Sickening James? Are you sure they are as bad as you make them sound? What have they done?"

"Well, James isn't *exactly* repulsive. I mean, that's just a word everyone's using at school right now, you know. But it isn't that, with James. I know what repulsive means. James is always sending away for things to places like New York and Chicago and San Francisco, trying to win prizes. He solves puzzles and things in comic magazines, but it seems he always has to sell something first before he can get his prize. I guess the selling part makes him gullible to win."

"I think you mean eligible, don't you?" her father suggested, adding, with a slight twinkle, "though certainly he is also gullible enough."

"Yes, eligible. Anyway, right now James has to sell two dozen ball-point pens to win a transistor radio or something. And Daddy, they really are very pretty pens. He has a lovely blue one that only costs a quarter and I do wish I could buy it — "

Both her parents laughed and Joanie wondered why. Then her mother said, "If you ask me, this James is a very enterprising young man. Some day he will be a very successful business man. At least he appears willing to work for what he wants, wouldn't you say?"

"So may I buy a pen, please? Just a quarter, Daddy?" Joanie's blue eyes were turned toward her father in appeal. She knew he could never resist this approach.

Mr. Sanders smiled, digging into his pocket to produce a coin. He tossed it across the room into Joanie's cupped hands. "Which brings us to Tommy-the-Monster. Let's hear about him so that we may turn to other things." He added, "But don't let it cost a quarter, young lady."

"Thanks, Daddy darling. I love you!" Joanie exulted. "And just you wait till you see the pen. Maybe you will want one too."

"I have my doubts," her father replied.

"Tommy, then. Well, there's a boy who is really impossible. I'm not the only one who thinks so, believe me." Joanie was once again self-righteous, indignant at the very thought of Tommy Mason. "He throws rocks. And he mimics the teacher behind her back. And he's mean as can be to caterpillars — "

"Caterpillars! Since when have you been championing crawling things?" Mr. Sanders exclaimed in surprise.

"It isn't that I like them exactly," Joanie explained. "But they do turn into butterflies and I like *them*. Besides, must you go around with a stick, squashing things?"

"But I don't," her father said.

"I know. But Tommy does. The squashier the better. Beetles he loves — for squashing only, of course. He never combs his hair, either. Or washes his hands or does anything at all that's civilized. Tommy's the worst."

"I'm sorry for the catepillars. Certainly Tommy doesn't sound too endearing, but one is free to ignore such goings-on. Now, may I return to my paper?"

Mrs. Sanders smiled at Joanie, her knitting needles starting to click away once again as she said, "Yes, darling — let Daddy read the news. I'm sure you have had your turn this evening."

Regretfully, Joanie went off to her room, unfinished homework suddenly on her mind.

SIX

THE FOLLOWING DAY WAS Saturday. Joanie helped her mother around the house for a time. Then, everything in order, her mother said, "Joanie dear, would you mind taking Danny for his outing today while I do the marketing? It would be so much easier for me to go alone."

"May I take him to the playground?" Joanie meant the school playground which was open to the children on Saturdays and where most of the younger set might be found. Usually, the boys had a ball game in progress and the girls found it fun to play volleyball or just get together to talk and make plans for picnics or parties. Sometimes they would watch the boys' baseball game and shout instructions, which failed to gain any recognition from the boys.

"You may, if you promise to keep careful watch over him at all times and not get him too close to the ball game," replied Mrs. Sanders. "I won't take more than an hour or so for the marketing, so you can bring Danny home after a while. And put on a coat — it isn't too warm outdoors today."

While her mother dressed Danny for the outing, Joanie got herself ready and presently she was wheeling his buggy onto the playground. There was only a handful of girls there and none of the girls were well known to Joanie. She felt a little disappointed and wandered around aimlessly, giving Danny an occasional absent smile when he made gurgling noises. She would have liked to watch the ball game — for the game's sake, of course, and not the players' — but she remembered her mother's admonitions concerning Danny's safety. So she perched herself on the deserted roundabout, digging the toe of her shoe into the ground beneath her. She hoped someone would come along pretty soon — this was really Dullsville! With Danny ready to fall asleep, she wondered whether she might dare leave him over by the fence for a little while. She decided against it and, for lack of anything more exciting to do, she set the roundabout in motion.

She had made no more than two rounds when she heard someone call her name. She looked around eagerly. Instinctively, she placed a finger to her lips to warn whoever it was that Danny was sleeping. Then she saw that it was Tommy Mason who had called her. A fat lot Tommy would care that her baby brother was sleeping! She doubled her fists and said, "Don't you dare wake the baby or I'll — "

"Who wants to wake him?" Tommy asked, with an impudent grin.

"He screams his head off when he's wakened suddenly," Joanie warned, her fists still clenched.

"Aw, so let him scream! It won't be me that wakes him up. All I wanted to do was offer you a gumdrop, but if you're going to be like that, forget it." He began to saunter away in the direction of the ball field.

64

"Gumdrops? Are you kidding?" Joanie couldn't believe Tommy's sudden generosity. She eyed with suspicion the paper sack he carried.

Tommy paused, opened the sack, and put his hand inside. He brought forth a licorice gumdrop, her favorite flavor, and popped it into his mouth. "Sure are good," he said.

"I'll take one." Joanie was unable to resist the temptation in spite of her dislike for Tommy. Maybe, after all, he was just trying to be friendly. Then she saw Tommy's hands, grubby as ever, and came close to declining the proffered candy. But she did love gumdrops, and since they were still in the sack and he was allowing her to help herself, she saw no reason to deny herself. She dipped her hand into the sack and, as she did so, Tommy grasped her wrist so that her hand was imprisoned in it. Then he began to laugh. Too late she realized this was nothing more than one of Tommy's practical jokes and she grew red with anger.

"Gumdrops! Gumdrops! Nice, squirmy, wriggly gumdrops!" Tommy chanted, while Joanie became unhappily aware of things crawling over her imprisoned hand. Wet, slimy, frightening things that only a monster like Tommy Mason would dare even to touch!

She began to scream, Danny forgotten completely. Even when the baby wakened and joined her in the screaming she did not notice, for cold fear held her in its grip. Only later did she remember that Tommy had said it would not be he who wakened Danny. She struggled in vain to free her hand from Tommy's strong hold on it, while all the time he laughed hilariously at her fright.

"I'll kill you, I will!" she sobbed, and screamed again. Others, hearing the screams, came running.

The first to arrive on the scene was Eric. At sight of him, Tommy immediately released Joanie's wrist. Joanie felt such a surge of gratitude toward her rescuer that she was rendered completely silent. Still shaken, all she could do was breathe deeply and give Eric a look of great relief.

During all the excitement the paper sack had fallen to the ground. Looking down at it now, Joanie saw two or three long, slithery worms crawl out. She began to scream again, wringing her hands helplessly as though shaking off even the memory of the worms' touch on her flesh.

Other boys had arrived, but it was Eric who took over after Tommy had exclaimed, in great disgust, "Screamy Mimi! Like she was being killed! Girls! Can't take a joke — "

Eric said loudly, "Shut up!"

Joanie stared at Eric, dumbfounded. He, of all people, to tell someone to shut up!

But Tommy did not shut up. Defiantly he said, "Sissy-girl! 'Fraid of a few harmless old worms! Honest, I thought she'd just laugh! How'd I know she'd be scared?"

Several of the boys were grinning, obviously amused. One of them said to Joanie, "Gosh, we thought someone was being murdered at the very least! Honest!"

Haughtily, Joanie retorted, "And well I might have been. People die of shock, in case you didn't know. He said they were gumdrops!" Again she turned on Tommy, her eyes still wet with tears. "I hate you, Tommy

Mason! I absolutely hate you!"

"Hey, your baby's crying," someone told her, and she guiltily started to push the buggy back and forth in a rhythmic motion, hoping to lull Danny back to sleep.

Tommy said, "'Fraidy-cat! I never saw such a 'fraidy-cat. Girls!" He picked up the worms and replaced them in the sack, adding, "I'm goin' fishin'."

Joanie tucked Danny's covers around him and started off for home. Boys! Of them all, only Eric had really shown any respect for her! As she trundled the buggy, she talked indignantly of the occurrence to Danny, whose nap had been completely disrupted by all the rumpus. That young man lay placidly sucking his thumb while she told him, "I'm sure you couldn't help being born a boy, Danny, but I hope you learned something from this today. I hope you have made up your mind not to do any of the horrid things you saw done to me!"

Danny said, "Goo-oo," and smiled sweetly.

Joanie arrived home in record time and found that her mother had just returned from her shopping trip. Surely more than an hour had passed! "Here's your son, Mother," she said, lifting Danny from the buggy and handing him to Mrs. Sanders. Her grimacing face caused her mother to ask, "Was he a bother, dear?"

"Not really," Joanie admitted, adding, "he cried a lot, but it really wasn't his fault, it was the other boys. They woke him from his nap. Tommy, in particular. So help me, Mother, if that Tommy Mason ever crosses my path again, I'll — I'll — oh!" She could not continue, angry tears filled her eyes and she brushed them away impatiently.

"Darling, what happened?" her mother asked, in some alarm.

"Tommy," Joanie sobbed. "He — he trapped my hand in a — a sackful of *worms!*" Sympathy always made her cry harder and for a few moments she was unable to go on. But finally she added, "He — he offered me candy and — and — "

"That was cruel," her mother said, "but maybe he didn't realize how you feel about worms, dear."

"Oh, didn't he? You should have heard him laugh!"

"Yes, but after he realized you were truly frightened?"

"He enjoyed it. He meant to frighten me. He just goes around dreaming up things to scare people and hurt them," Joanie declared, convinced of Tommy's treacherous nature.

"It isn't easy to know what really goes on in someone else's mind, dear. I'm sure Tommy's joy was short-lived once he saw how the other boys felt about his behavior," Mrs. Sanders commented.

"But golly, that's just it! They thought nothing of it, Mother. I mean, no one patted him on the back, of course, but they did seem to think I was being a baby. Well, I'll get even with Tommy and I don't care what anyone thinks. The sooner I get promoted to Fifth, the better. I'm going to study like a fiend! I might even wind up in Sixth — or Seventh — "

"My goodness, not so fast!" Mrs. Sanders was laughing. She remembered some candy she had bought at the market. The fact that the candy was gumdrops somewhat lessened Joanie's enthusiasm for it, however. She ate only three pieces.

SEVEN

ONE MORNING TOWARD THE end of October, after roll-call and the Pledge of Allegiance, Miss Coles smiled at the children and announced, "I have something lovely to tell you, boys and — " Everyone giggled, knowing she had been about to say "girls." "Boys and girl," she amended, sharing their amusement. "We are going to plan a play for the Christmas season!"

One or two groans greeted this announcement, indicating that her announcement was not creating any great ethusiasm. But, undaunted, Miss Coles went on, "This isn't going to be an ordinary, read-from-a-book sort of play. We are going to have rehearsals and costumes, and you, all of you, are to select the play yourselves. Every grade in the school will do the same thing and there is to be a prize for the best play given."

Faces brightened a little. A prize was always something to take into account. Then James raised his hand and asked, "But Miss Coles, will we have a chance against all the upper grades?"

"Yes, indeed," the teacher answered. "The plays will be judged with the ages of the players in mind."

"What's the prize?" James asked.

He would, Joanie thought with disdain. James loved prizes.

"Oh, something really exciting. I'm sure, when you hear about it, you will all want to do your best to put on a fine play. The reward will be a trip to the Planetarium in Griffith Park in Los Angeles. All expenses will be paid, including the bus fares and lunches."

It was unbelievable! Tommy said no one in the world could afford to pay for a whole grade to go to Griffith Park. Why, Los Angeles was over a hundred miles away from Briarcliff Lake! "Anyway," he concluded, "what is a platternaria — plantatarion?"

"Class, who can tell Tommy what a planetarium is? Who can spell it? Yes, Joanie?" Miss Coles nodded in response to Joanie's upshot hand.

"I can spell it," Joanie said. "P-l-a-n-e-t-a-r-i-u-m, planetarium."

Archie's hand was also raised and, after Joanie's correct spelling had received acknowledgement, he was invited to speak.

"The word is self-explanatory," Archie began, somewhat stuffily, Joanie thought. "We all know what a planet is, of course. So a planetarium is a sort of apparatus — "

"What's that?" Tommy was being quite difficult. Miss Coles gave him a severe glance and told Archie to continue.

"Well, in *simple* language, a planetarium shows us how the stars and planets move in their orbits and you can sort of get an idea as to how the universe really is. I know it sounds quite dull, but I have been to the Hayden Planetarium in New York with my father, and it is very exciting, really it is. Also, it is very educational, and I think we would be very fortunate to win such a prize, Miss Coles."

"Thank you, Archie. You did a splendid job of explaining. As to who will be paying for the trip, I would like to tell you that the local Chamber of Commerce is sponsoring the contest. We are very fortunate to have a civic group so interested in us, aren't we?" Miss Coles added.

Everyone began talking at once now. They had to win, they all agreed. They simply must win this tremendous prize! During the noisy chatter, Miss Coles took time to arrange some papers on her desk but finally called for order.

"The play will be presented during the Christmas season, of course," she said, "so we have plenty of time to rehearse. The immediate problem is selecting the right play. Are there any suggestions?"

Bobby said, "Gosh, is there a play for nine boys and one girl?" He looked doubtfully around the room.

"It's a challenge," came Miss Coles' answer.

"Personally, I think it would be a lot more difficult to find a play for nine girls and one boy," Joanie commented. "Why, there are dozens and dozens of ideas for boys! Like *King Arthur and his Knights of the Round Table*, for instance. Or *Robin Hood* with all his Merry Men. Or — or —"

"We could do a Western," Jackie suggested, an enthusiastic gleam in his eye.

"Yeah! And if Joanie *has* to have a part, she could be an Indian maiden the cowboys have to rescue," Tommy said.

72

"Certainly Joanie has to have a part. You boys haven't overlooked how beautifully she reads, have you? But I doubt the sort of Western you have in mind, boys, is the type of play we are seeking," Miss Coles said, pointing to Eric, whose hand was raised.

"Both *King Arthur* and *Robin Hood* have parts for girls," he reminded the class. "There is Lady Guinevere and — "

"Oh, I'd like that," Joanie couldn't help interrupting.

"And Maid Marian," Eric continued, as though he hadn't heard Joanie.

"I'd like that, too." Joanie's enthusiasm was growing.

"Those are fine suggestions, I'll admit, but we must also keep in mind the scenery which would be necessary. And the costumes, too. We ought to keep them fairly simple," Miss Coles pointed out.

Archie suggested *Ivanhoe*.

Miss Coles gave this some consideration, then said, "The costumes would be just as difficult, I'm afraid. And the story is a little beyond our age group, wouldn't you say, Archie?"

Looking around at his classmates, Archie conceded, somewhat reluctantly, that perhaps she was right. Even though he, personally, had enjoyed reading *Ivanhoe*, he admitted it was a book on his father's bookshelf, not one from the suggested reading list for fourth graders.

Joanie, resenting Archie's attitude of superiority, said, "My father started to read *Ivanhoe* to me but I didn't like it too well. All that duelling and stuff! Miss Coles, couldn't we do *Snow White and the Seven*

73

Dwarfs? After all, the play is supposed to interest everyone, isn't it? Not just people our age and older?"

"Definitely! The audience is always the most important consideration. How about Joanie's suggestion, boys?" Miss Coles seemed pleased.

"She'd get the biggest part," someone objected.

"True. But it would mean the most work. Joanie would have a great many lines to memorize — though I'm sure she could do it."

"Could I be Doc, Miss Coles?" Damon asked, timidly.

"Aw, you couldn't remember a line even with only one word in it," Tommy told Damon unpleasantly.

It was true that Damon was not very bright, but Joanie felt it was very unkind to be so blunt about it. He couldn't help it, and he was the only boy in the class who didn't bother her.

"I want to be Happy," Mark shouted.

"Please, Miss Coles, may I be the huntsman who sets Snow White free?" asked Eric, his quiet voice a total contrast to Mark's.

"Wasn't it a prince who did that?" Bobby asked.

"I believe so, Bobby. However, we can settle that when we go through the story — it does look as though we are all just about agreed on doing *Snow White*. But let's take a vote on it. All in favor, raise your hands," Miss Coles suggested.

Promptly, every hand shot upward.

Suddenly, Chris seemed to remember something about the play. "Miss Coles, there are two parts for girls," he said.

"Oh dear me, yes. The wicked queen!" Miss Coles

agreed, looking dismayed. "I should have thought of that!"

Undaunted, Joanie said, "I'll do both parts."

The teacher considered this offer and then said, "Do you think you could, Joanie? It would be fine, but the trouble is, there will be a scene or two in which both characters appear together. How could we overcome that?"

James said, "In the movies they do that, sometimes. You remember *The Prince and the Pauper?*"

"The version I saw involved twins," Miss Coles told Chris. She added, "Of course, that was a long time ago. There have probably been other versions since. Still, I'm afraid we won't be equipped to perform what the movie-makers call camera tricks."

Suddenly Tommy jumped up, almost as though he'd been stuck with a pin. He waved his hand in the air, making sure Miss Coles would give him her attention. He seemed excited. "Miss Coles," he began, eagerly, "it wouldn't mean I was a sissy if I did the part of the wicked queen, would it? I mean, being so wicked and all! Actually, I don't think a girl could really act that wicked, do you? And she wouldn't want to be made up to look so ugly, anyway, I guess. Gosh, I bet I could make like a witch, all right! I bet witches were actually men in the first place — "

Joanie contemplated Tommy. She thought that if he wanted the only mean part in the play, he'd better have it! Tommy wouldn't have to act, he need only be himself! She said sweetly, "I'm sure Tommy could be mean enough, Miss Coles. But — he won't be allowed to do anything to — scare me on stage, will he?" It was plain that this last thought bothered her.

Miss Coles was reassuring. "It isn't likely Tommy would want to ruin our chances of winning the prize, is it, Joanie?"

Joanie shook her head in agreement and felt sorry she had said anything. She was glad to leave the room when Miss Coles suggested she run to the library down the hall to get a copy of *Snow White and the Seven Dwarfs* so that the class might review the story before the casting actually began.

After the children had looked the story over, they were surprised to discover that the dwarfs had no individual names — unless numbers one through seven constituted names. There was considerable disappointment in learning this, and, although Miss Coles would have preferred to stick by the original version of the story, she did agree that names so familiar to the children gave the little men endearing personalities.

"If Mr. Walt Disney could bring the story up to date with such success, I suppose there is nothing wrong in our borrowing the name idea from him," she said. "But I did want to call the matter to your attention. Today we see so many modernizations of charming old stories which actually spoil the original versions. I thought we should at least discuss this point."

The children nodded, then proceeded with the business of casting. Everyone agreed that because Archie was just about the nicest looking boy in the class, he should have the part of the prince. Archie was somewhat embarrassed by the compliment, but eagerly accepted the important role.

Someone giggled, then whispered, loud enough for

Joanie to hear, "Hey, the prince has to kiss Snow White!"

Joanie felt herself blushing. Still, if she must be kissed, she preferred Archie to any of the others. But maybe Miss Coles would do something about this.

Damon was finally persuaded to play the part of Bashful rather than that of Doc, for as Bashful he would have no lines to memorize. Bobby agreed to be Dopey, making a funny face to demonstrate his capacity for playing the role. Jack then showed the class how well he could produce a realistic sneeze, thus assuring himself of the role of Sneezy.

Chris, because his father was a real doctor, was the unanimous choice for Doc, while his twin, Mark, was given the part he had first asked for, that of Happy.

"Chris is the serious twin and Mark is the laughing one, so it works out just right," Joanie approved.

The role of Sleepy fell to James Tate, who stated flatly that he couldn't perform well and wanted only a very small part. There was only one other role to be filled. Yes, indeed, there was a huntsman! Eric looked so grateful on learning the part was his, Joanie thought, that even had there been no such character in the story one should have been created for him.

Presently Miss Coles glanced at the clock and said, "Well, we can't afford to spend any more time today on the play, so let us get on with our lessons. Tomorrow, during Language period, we will start rehearsals. But now, everyone take out his arithmetic book, please, and turn to page thirty-five."

Because the day's beginning had been so pleasant, it was recess time before anyone realized it. On the playground, Joanie found herself to be the most envied girl in school. No matter what play her class had selected, the other girls commented enviously, Joanie was assured the leading feminine role. For the first time since starting Briarcliff Lake School, Joanie admitted to an advantage in being the only girl in her grade. She was remembering, too, with secret pleasure, a remark Chris had made — that they were lucky Joanie was so pretty. A girl who wasn't pretty wouldn't make a very suitable Snow White. And Eric had mentioned her excellence in reading, a fact which, in his mind at least, would assure the Fourth grade of a successful performance.

EIGHT

ANOTHER WEEK PASSED AND rehearsals were well under way. Miss Coles decided, however, that once the play showed promise of running smoothly, they had better devote more time to lessons. Most of the children had been practising their lines at home as well as at school, so Miss Coles felt little doubt that, when the time came, they would all give a splendid performance.

"Today I thought you might like to learn something about poetry," she told the class. "Not memorizing poetry but the composition of it. We are going to consider the subject of rhyming as compared to rhythm. The two are not at all the same. Who knows what rhyming means?"

Three hands went up, Joanie's, Archie's and Eric's. Miss Coles pointed to Eric and Archie dropped his hand with a disappointed sigh. Joanie was glad Eric had been called on. Archie knew everything!

"It's like when two words sound almost the same," Eric explained.

"For example?" Miss Coles encouraged him, smiling.

"Well, like smoke and choke," Eric replied, and several boys laughed.

The teacher pointed to one of them. "He's perfectly correct, Bobby. But since you find it so amusing, how about giving us two lines of poetry, using these words?"

Bobby considered the matter and then said brightly, "Holy smoke, I thought I'd choke!" He sat down, amidst laughter.

Miss Coles called for quiet. "There," she stated, when the room subsided. "We are led straight to the point I wanted to make. Bobby has rhymed, but there was no rhythm to the lines. I am not going to ask any of you to tell me what rhythm is just now. Instead, I want you all to compose a short poem. Then we will analyze each one and — "

"What does *analyze* mean?" Jack interrupted.

"Does anyone know?" the teacher inquired. This time Archie was the only one with an answer.

He said, "It means to sort of take apart, to study each little detail."

Joanie nodded her head emphatically to indicate that she had known the answer all the time.

Miss Coles said they might start their poems at once. They could write about anything at all, she added, as, one by one, pencils became busy. The faces of the children reflected their thoughts. Archie's was deliberate and thoughtful. Bobby's eyes were closed in deep concentration. Tommy chewed on the end of his pencil, and Damon simply sat with a glazed look which offered no clue to his reaction to the task at hand.

Joanie felt little confidence in her own ability to write a really good poem, but she thought she could rhyme words well enough. She knew what rhythm meant, too, and that, she felt sure, would surprise and

80

please the teacher. With this encouraging thought, she smiled to herself and began to write,

Squirrel with your bushy tail,
To feed you I must never fail.

She found it difficult to complete the verse. She bit her lip, determined to finish at any cost, and presently went on,

Even though I am late for school
To feed you first must be my rule.

She laid down her pencil and sat back with a sense of triumph. She had remembered, she congratulated herself silently, that the first letter of every line in a poem is capitalized. Her father had once told her that, and she doubted that anyone else in the class knew it, including Archie!

"Finished already, Joanie?" Miss Coles asked, surprised.

"Yes, Miss Coles." Joanie tried to sound modest.

Miss Coles looked doubtful and suggested, "We still have five more minutes — time to improve, if you feel you can, Joanie."

"Yes, Miss Coles," Joanie answered, taking up her pencil politely. She was sure she had done a good job, but she turned her eyes upward in an effort to appear deep in concentration, while Miss Coles turned her attention to someone else. Damon, it was obvious, needed encouragement.

Presently the time was up and the pupils were told to put down their pencils.

"Eric, will you read your poem for us, please?"

Eric, a smile of satisfaction upon his pleasant face, rose and began to read,

"I have a dog, his name is Pat,
He ran away with my father's hat.
The end."

He sat down without looking at anyone.

"Why Eric, that was very good! Now Jack, you may read yours." Miss Coles smiled encouragingly.

"Y-yes, Miss Coles. I — I — oh, darn it, I can't write any poems, Miss Coles!" Jack fidgeted unhappily.

"That's all right, Jack. How about — " Miss Coles was about to name someone else when Chris begged, "Please, Miss Coles, can't I read mine before the bell rings?"

"The bell isn't about to ring for some time, Chris, but of course we may not get to everyone today. If you have a good poem — why yes, let us hear it." Miss Coles seemed surprised, for Chris was one of the quieter pupils in the class.

Chris smiled and began,

"A puppy's fur, a kitten's tongue,
I love anything that's young.
I have a cat, I have a lamb,
What a lucky boy I am!"

"Good! Class, wasn't that a lovely poem?" Miss Coles looked very pleased, even proud.

Joanie thought it was lovely too. She couldn't understand how a boy could write such a gentle sort of poem. She had expected most of them to write about cowboys or shooting or exploring.

Then Miss Coles called upon Tommy. Joanie sat at attention. His very first words were an indication of what might follow.

"It's about something," he said, "that happened on

82

the playground . . . Poem:

> Once there was a girl named Joan
> Fell upon a tiny stone.
> The way she cried
> We thought she'd died — "

Tommy gulped as though on the verge of laughing, and finished,

> "Or at least broke her funnybone!"

He sat down abruptly, convulsed with laughter.

Miss Coles' eyes expressed a measure of amusement, but her voice was stern as she said, "Well, Tommy, I must admit you have a sense of rhyme, even though the rhythm could be improved. However, your subject matter is most unkind. I think you had better apologize to Joanie at once, since I gather you are referring to her."

Several boys were snickering by this time, but Miss Coles' displeasure was a warning that brought them to order quickly. Joanie, her face burning, listened to Tommy's muttered, "I apologize, Joanie — " Then she burst out fiercely, "Don't ever say you're sorry when you don't mean it, Tommy Mason! It only makes things worse!" She blinked back angry tears, vowing not to give Tommy the added satisfaction of seeing her cry. She composed herself while Mark read his poem and, when she was called upon, rose without hesitation.

But suddenly she realized her poem was not outstanding. The other poems were so surprisingly good that she was now reluctant to read hers. This fact, added to her hurt over Tommy's offering, caused her to say honestly, "Mine isn't really a very good poem, Miss Coles."

"But this isn't a contest, Joanie. I'm sure you did your best, just as the others tried to do. Go ahead, please."

"Well then — " Joanie read her poem, then went on to explain, not without pride, "I capitalized the first letter of each line, Miss Coles. Would you like to see — ?"

Miss Coles' reaction was adequate and Joanie felt better.

The bell rang and several of the boys who had not been called on seemed happy to escape.

School was over for the day and Joanie hurried off as quickly as she could. She wanted to get as far away from the boys as possible. They not only thought her a crybaby but by now they were probably considering her prissy and sentimental because of her poem. Chris's verse was every bit as sentimental, but naturally the boys wouldn't think anything about it because it had been written by one of them. She decided to walk the distance between school and home instead of taking the bus. Once aboard the bus the boys would begin to tease her since they would be outside the teacher's domain.

If she walked swiftly the distance wouldn't seem long. It was a lovely day. She felt cosy and warm in a new ski suit.

She had gone only a few steps beyond the school grounds when she heard someone behind her call her name. Almost at once Archie was at her side. "Mind if I walk with you? My father said I ought to walk home on nice days to get the exercise. He says we kids are too pampered." Archie sounded as though his father were the world's wisest man.

Joanie shrugged. "I just wanted to be by myself," she told him, adding, for fear she sounded insulting, "but it's all right if you want to walk too. It's Tommy I'm mad at, really. And the others who laughed at his poem. I just didn't want to listen to any more smart-alecky talk on the bus — "

"It wasn't very nice of Tommy, that's true. But golly, Joanie, the others have probably forgotten it by now. And anyway, Tommy doesn't ride our bus."

Why did Archie always manage to make her feel slightly ridiculous? Joanie wondered. Without intending to, of course.

Her silence must somehow have conveyed her feelings to Archie, for he said, "You know, Joanie, it isn't just you, with Tommy. He seems to have it in for all girls. It's just too bad that you happen to be the only girl around for him to pick on."

"Well, I've got news for you — and Tommy. I hate all boys. So I guess that makes us even, Tommy and me."

Archie stared, disbelieving, his eyeglasses flashing in the sunlight. "*All* boys, Joanie? Even me?" he asked.

Impulsively, Joanie said, "Well no, not you." And

then she knew it was simply good manners which had prompted her words. Or was it? After a moment, she added, thoughtfully, "No, I guess I don't hate you, Archie. You don't tease me. You treat me just the way you treat the boys, as though it makes no difference to you that I'm a girl."

Archie blinked and then smiled. They reached his house first and, by the time they parted, Joanie felt quite friendly toward him. For the remainder of her walk home, she went through her lines for the play, speaking out loud, for there was no one around to hear and perhaps to think her slightly mad. When she came to the part in the play where the prince arrives on the scene, she paused to murmur to herself, "Wouldn't it be perfectly poisonous to have anyone else but Archie playing the prince!"

Naturally, she told her parents about Tommy's most recent outrage, again expressing her indignation and the hope that he would be, as she termed it, "good and sorry one of these days."

Her father commented, "Seems to me your boy-hating is centering more and more upon one boy in particular, Joanie."

"One monster in particular," she corrected him, adding vehemently, "but you needn't think I like all the others. At best, they're repulsive. Except, maybe Archie, who still isn't — well, he's Archie."

"I see. But Joanie, when a boy — or a girl, for that matter — behaves as Tommy does, there is usually some reason for it. Perhaps one of these days you will discover what makes Tommy tick. In the meantime, do try to take these things a bit more — well — try to control your feelings a little. After all, Tommy isn't the beginning and the end, you know."

"Maybe not," Joanie retorted with spirit, "but he certainly tries to be everything in the middle!" She was remembering the worm episode.

There were no other outstanding incidents during the next few weeks. Time went by in comparative peace for the girl who felt the world would be a much happier place in which to live if there were no boys to inhabit it. For one thing, the play was occupying much of Joanie's time and thought.

Thanksgiving and the promise of snow were now imminent. Taking her place at the breakfast table one morning, Joanie said, her teeth chattering, "Daddy, are you *sure* this is California and not Alaska? I'm freezing!"

Mr. Sanders was busy laying a fire in the huge stone fireplace, one of two which the house boasted. "At an altitude of 7,500 feet, cold is to be expected," her father answered her. "Still, I'd hardly confuse this with Alaska. This weather is wonderful — crisp, exhilarating — makes one glad to be alive." He rubbed his hands together in high spirits. Then he sniffed the air — which, to Joanie, smelled only of bacon and smoke from the kindling — and said, "Snow in the air, or I miss my guess."

"Snow!" Instantly, Joanie's eyes shone with joy. But her obvious pleasure might have been called somewhat deceptive. Not that she wasn't eager to see snow; however, its promise suggested a pleasure concerned solely with revenge. She had thought of it some time ago, when the first mention of snow was made. The coming of snow could mean getting even with Tommy Mason. It did seem a pity, she was ready to admit to herself, that her very first snowball fight would be for the purpose of revenge. Yet she was sure nothing would bring her greater satisfaction. She would simply creep up on Tommy from behind and pelt him with snowballs. They wouldn't really hurt him, except his pride. And that was all she cared about hurting. Just as he'd hurt hers. All the boys would laugh to see a girl get a rise out of Tommy!

"How's the play coming along?" Mr. Sanders' voice brought Joanie back to the breakfast table.

"Oh, just fine," she answered. "We are to present ours at the P.T.A. meeting in December. You see, there are eight grades competing, so of course the plays can't all be given at the same time." She laughed at the absurdity of the idea and went on, "There will be a play given at almost every gathering during the month — at least at every one which all the judges will be able to attend. Getting them together at the same time seems to be giving everyone the most trouble right now. All the judges are important people, you see. There may have to be two plays given at each meeting. Anyway, that is for the grownups to settle."

Mrs. Sanders said, "At the last P.T.A. meeting it was suggested that two of the plays be given at the Chamber of Commerce Christmas party, two at the Country Club dinner, two at the next P.T.A. meeting — yours, for one, Joanie, as you know — and the last two at some affair the Kiwanians are to have. That seemed to exhaust the possibilities so far as the judges' time and availability are concerned."

Mr. Sanders grinned, "I'm glad I'm not to be a judge. I declined on the grounds that I might be a little biased in favor of my own talented daughter."

"Oh, Daddy, you wouldn't! Most likely, you'd be more critical of our play than the others, just to be fair. I know you! Still, I'm glad you refused, because all the kids would be expecting us to win — and just imagine what it would be like for me if we didn't!" Joanie turned to her mother and said, "You *will* have my costume ready, won't you, Mother?"

"Darling, don't worry. It will be ready for a fitting today, after school." Mrs. Sanders glanced at the clock and exclaimed, "My goodness, look at the time! Eat your breakfasts, you two, or you'll be late for school. The eggs must be stone cold!" She hesitated over the scrambled eggs as though she intended to do something about warming them, but a wail from Danny's room caused her to hurry off. When she returned with the baby, all bundled up in a woolly blue robe, she saw that the eggs were half gone.

Joanie watched her mother put Danny in his high chair and start to feed him. He looked so rosy and cuddly! Impossible to believe he would grow into one of those *characters!* But of course he would, for one could not change the plain facts. It was just Danny's misfortune to have been born a boy.

NINE

"HEY, JOANIE, WAKE UP! Look out the window!" Her father's gay voice wakened Joanie from a warm, comfortable dream in which she was drifting over Briarcliff Lake on a downy cloud of orange blossoms. She stirred, yawned, stretched, and called sleepily, "Go away!" She closed her eyes again. The dream was gone, however, and the sensation of cold, as from a chill draft, became a reality. She sat up, hating the thought of running across the room to shut the window when it was so comfortable under the bed clothes. Then someone opened the door.

Guiltily, she protested, "I'm up — " and scrambled for her robe.

"Put your slippers on," her mother said from the doorway. She added, "Do look out of the window, Joanie!" Mrs. Sanders hurried across the room to open the shutters and to shut tight the upper sash. Joanie was beside her almost instantly.

"O-oh! Oh, is that snow, Mother? Oh, how perfectly wonderfully beautiful! Look at the trees, Mother! They're beautiful!"

"Joanie! Shut the window! You'll catch a cold!" was her mother's reply.

90

Joanie slammed the sash down again instantly. She laughed, "I just wanted to touch the snow on the sill to make sure it's real." She began at once to get into her clothes. She shivered as she did so and her mother turned up the heater, murmuring that the heating system in the house could be improved upon. She left the room.

In the bathroom, Joanie found the water icy cold; only a dribble came through the faucet. Obviously there was no hot water. She decided that no one could expect her to take a shower under such conditions. Even to brush her teeth seemed to be asking a little too much. How could she eat, if her teeth were frozen? It would be better to have a decayed tooth or two, she said aloud, than to die of starvation. Thus deciding, she finished dressing and raced downstairs.

"May I go out right away?" she asked, excitement lighting her eyes.

"Daddy's already out there, shovelling a path from the house to the garage. Maybe you would like to help him?" her mother replied, busy at the sink. "Dear me, no hot water — " she sighed, jiggling the faucet hopelessly.

Joanie donned her coat, stuffing the matching red mittens into her pocket. In her haste she completely forgot the red galoshes, bought for her only a week ago in anticipation of just such a morning as this. Then, pushing open the back door, she immediately plunged into two feet of soft snow. A booby trap if ever there was one! She shivered in surprise as she felt the cold wetness against her bare legs. She promptly retreated to the warm kitchen, the bottom of her damp coat and dress flapping unpleasantly around her legs. She had never been so conscious of her legs before! Two columns of ice! She was surprised to see, upon looking at them, that they were almost as red as her mittens. Her legs should have been blue! And how they tingled! She laughed gaily.

Mrs. Sanders shook her head in mock despair. "Better get into something dry at once," she advised, looking askance at the dress she had ironed only the day before. "Why didn't you put on your ski suit? Take off those shoes! And please, not a cotton dress on a day like this! A skirt and pullover, for goodness' sake!"

"I'm sorry, Mother — I was in such a hurry to go out." Joanie hastened to her room to dress more appropriately. Soon she was back outdoors, whooping and screaming and laughing as her father scooped up handfuls of snow and threw them at her. He was having the time of his life, Joanie decided. Mountains of snow banked each side of the driveway and Joanie's belated offer to help shovel a path was hardly necessary. Mr. Sanders, it appeared, had been shovelling since dawn.

"I think I've earned a snowball fight!" he declared, suiting action to the word by hurling a fast one in her direction.

It was fun! Daddy acting like a crazy boy — laughing and yelling just like one of his own students! What if any of them should happen by and see him? Joanie had a glimpse, for a moment, of what he must have been like long before she was born. A boy — bent on knocking her head off! Oh, dear — *no!* What was she thinking of? This was Daddy! Daddy, wanting her to have fun in the snow with him. Still, upon remembering why she had so longed for this day, she felt compelled to call, "Please, Daddy, no more fighting!"

"Chicken!" he teased, "Who's fighting? Aren't you enjoying it?" He dropped the soft ball of snow he had poised, ready to throw.

"Oh, yes," Joanie made haste to assure him. "But — but, well, couldn't we just sort of make a snow man now?" She swallowed, then added quietly, "I — I can't hit *you!*"

"Why not? That would be fun!" Mr. Sanders began at once to roll an immense ball of snow, giving Joanie a brief glance that was slightly disturbing.

He must know what she was thinking! Mean thoughts had no place on a pure white morning like this. Oh, if only she had never met Tommy Mason! It was all his fault! But she had to follow through, she couldn't help herself.

Mr. Sanders was now giving his full attention to fashioning the snow man. He told Joanie to fetch a carrot and some bits of charcoal, for the snow man's features. "Bring that old felt hat of mine, too, the one I wear when I'm sweeping up the garage," he added, lifting an enormous snow head onto the broad shoulders of the snow man's body. Once finished, it stood as high as its creator, and was four times his girth.

Presently, Mrs. Sanders called the two in to breakfast. She immediately served them steaming hot bowls of oatmeal with rich cream and golden honey.

"Ah, a breakfast worthy of the weather!" sighed Mr. Sanders, who appeared to be irrepressible this morning.

It seemed to Joanie that the day should be at least half over by the time she was finally on her way to the school bus. The road was not the stretch of immaculate whiteness she had expected. Passing cars had churned the snow to slush and she had to dodge the splashings each time a vehicle went by. She found herself wishing she had ridden in the car with her father, as he had suggested — especially at the moment when she slipped and landed, sitting upright, in the middle of a slushy puddle. Her lovely blue ski suit was quite a mess.

Undaunted, she scrambled to her feet and hurried on. The tumble had given her an idea. If slushy and soft, the snowballs she meant to hurl at Tommy would be far

94

more effective. All she need do was hurl them hard enough, making sure of her aim, to her target, the back of Tommy's neck. They would slide down under his collar, melt, and trickle down his spine! She would make him wriggle and holler. She would treat him the way he liked to treat her! Joanie enjoyed these thoughts all the way to school.

She saw Tommy almost as soon as she entered the school grounds. He was easily recognizable because of the big red demon emblem on the back of his jacket. The jacket had first belonged to his older brother and, had it not been for the emblem, Joanie felt sure Tommy would have resented having to wear it. But the emblem was that of a football team made up of older boys and Tommy fondly hoped he might be taken for one of them by wearing it. The jacket looked ridiculous, Joanie thought, for it was at least two sizes too large for Tommy and made him look like a pigmy.

Tommy was standing still, his back toward Joanie. Perfect! She stooped down, scooped up a handful of melting snow, and, getting close enough to Tommy to assure a direct hit, threw the snowball for all she was worth. *Wham!* Right between where his bright green scarf met the edge of his cap! If Tommy's head had not been slightly bowed over something Jack was showing him, the snowball might not have touched his skin at all. But, as Tommy's back suddenly stiffened and he swung around, Joanie knew she had hit her target! Oh, how mad he looked! Wriggling and jumping around, he looked for all the world like a corkscrew winding its way into a bottle! He was slapping at the back of his neck and growling vengeance on his unknown assailant.

Satisfied at last, Joanie turned away and found a few girls with whom to have fun until the bell rang.

Later, in class, Joanie stole a glance in Tommy's direction. He was calm, and she began to wonder if one measly old snowball could really be considered sufficient punishment for him. Perhaps she ought to think of something else to do to him. Suddenly, into the silence of the room, came a loud, emphatic sneeze, its noise filling the air like the sound of a discordant trumpet. The sneeze was followed immediately by another, even larger sneeze, and Joanie discovered, along with the rest of the class, that they came from Tommy.

Miss Coles took a handful of tissues from her desk drawer and hastily presented them to Tommy. "My goodness, are you catching cold, Tommy?" she asked, in some concern.

"Id seebs like id, Biss Coles," Tommy replied heavily.

"Let me feel your forehead," the teacher said, while the others watched with interest. Any interruption was interesting, especially during spelling.

Miss Coles had placed a cool hand upon Tommy's forehead. "You seem to have a slight temperature, Tommy," she said. "I think you had better see the nurse right away."

With alacrity, Tommy hurried off. Spelling was not Tommy's favorite subject. Within a few minutes, however, he was back. His flushed face was wreathed in smiles as he announced, "The durse says for be to go hobe, Biss Coles, ad go to bed." Tommy was obviously delighted with this unexpected turn of events.

96

Joanie had watched and listened to all this in silence. A feeling of guilt stirred within her. Why? Could she and her snowball have had anything to do with Tommy's cold? Mother *had* scolded her this morning for opening the window and also for getting herself wet and cold. She had said Joanie could catch a dreadful cold if she wasn't careful. But a snowball? Hadn't she and Daddy tossed dozens of them at each other? Ah, but this had been different. It had hit Tommy right smack on his bare neck — and where else is a cold centered? Maybe not in the neck, but pretty close to it!

As the morning progressed, Joanie became more and more disturbed. Twice she failed to respond when called upon. At noon, when the others bemoaned the fact that the snow seemed to be melting fast and their fun along with it, Joanie felt utterly disinterested. She couldn't care less, she told herself.

Tommy failed to return to school the following day. The day after that, news reached the class that Tommy Mason was in the hospital, suffering from pneumonia.

At dinner that evening, Joanie toyed with her dessert, after eating only a small portion of meat and vegetables. She had hardly spoken a word throughout the meal and when Danny turned his cereal bowl upside down on top of his head, she made no comment. Ordinarily, she would have said something like, "Aren't you ever going to learn any manners, Danny Sanders? How revolting!"

Her silence aroused her father's curiosity at last. For Joanie to let Danny's prank go unnoticed was certainly cause for parental alarm! "Something wrong with your chocolate pudding?" he asked.

"Huh? Oh, no. It's really very nice. Only I — I'm just not very hungry tonight, I guess."

"Darling, don't you feel well? So much flu going — " Mrs. Sanders was concerned.

"I feel all right," Joanie mumbled.

"*Something's* wrong," her father insisted, eyeing her rather intently. "You haven't been eating too well for the last two days, come to think of it. You aren't worrying about the play, are you, Princess?"

"You love chocolate pudding with a smidgen of mint, usually," her mother said, looking quite upset.

Almost inaudibly, Joanie blurted out, "Tommy Mason's in the hospital. He has pneumonia."

"Oh? Well, that's a shame — but why should you be so shaken, Joanie? I mean, well, Tommy Mason? He's your direst enemy, isn't he?" Mr. Sanders added, in a warmer tone, "I certainly hope it isn't very serious."

"I said, *he's in the hospital*," Joanie answered ominously.

"Oh. Yes. Then I suppose he really must be quite ill," her mother commented sympathetically.

Tears filled Joanie's eyes at the very hint of sympathy. She moaned, "I'm a monster! I did it, Mother! I gave Tommy pneumonia! Oh Mother — Daddy — !"

"Joanie, that's absurd. You don't have pneumonia — and it isn't contagious, anyway. So how in the world do you figure — ?"

"I did, j-just the same. And supposing he d-dies? I'll have k-killed Tommy! Oh Mother, I d-didn't hate him *that* much! What can I *do?*" The tears coursed down Joanie's cheeks unchecked as she looked imploringly at her parents.

98

Consternation greeted her outburst. "Joanie, darling, why don't you just tell us about it? Start right at the beginning and maybe it will make sense to us." Mrs. Sanders' voice was sympathetic and encouraging.

So Joanie told her parents how Tommy's constant needling had finally reached the point where she simply had to retaliate in some way. "He did mean things to me for no reason at all, Mother. How could I help hating him when he was always being so horrible toward me? I just kept getting madder and madder at Tommy, that's all. And when the snow came, I thought it was my chance to get even. I slammed him real hard in the back of his neck with a snowball. How was I to know? But I'm sorry it turned out the way it did, and I just don't know what to do!" Joanie had reached the point of hysteria as she buried her face in her mother's shoulder.

Mr. Sanders came over to her and lifted her face in his hands, his voice filled with concern. "Joanie, dear — the truth, now — you didn't, by any chance, have a rock in the snowball?"

"A rock?" Joanie was definitely puzzled.

"I apologize. I didn't really think so, but I had to be sure. So, darling, how do you figure you gave Tommy pneumonia? Frankly, I think the young monkey deserved more than a soft snowball, though of course I'm sorry he's in the hospital."

"Well, I'm glad you're on my side," Joanie said, a faint smile brightening her face a little. "I mean, it wasn't that I meant anything worse than to show him I'd *had* it. But that very morning he began to sniffle and sneeze and had to be sent home. Oh Daddy, what can I do? People die of pneumonia, don't they?" Fear

99

had returned to Joanie's eyes. Her mother patted her head comfortingly. Joanie sat waiting for her father to answer her.

"There was a time when it was a frightening thing to have pneumonia. But today, with all the marvelous antibiotics and other wonder drugs, it is no longer considered the dread illness it once was. As a matter of fact, the last time I went to Doctor Harkness with a bad cold, he told me, jokingly, to catch pneumonia instead, because there was a cure for that and there still was none for a cold! Fortunately, I managed to recover in spite of him!"

Her father's humor was meant to cheer her, Joanie knew. He returned to his chair and the cup of coffee cooling on the table.

"Still, pneumonia's bad, isn't it?" Joanie persisted.

"Certainly it isn't anything to cheer about," Mr. Sanders admitted, grimacing over the coffee and setting the cup down. As his wife was about to offer a fresh cupful, he rose abruptly and put down his napkin. "Come Joanie. We're about to pay a call," he said.

As he ushered Joanie toward the hall and their coats, Mrs. Sanders said, "It's really no wonder the boy is ill, the way those Mason children are allowed to do exactly as they please. There is a houseful of youngsters and, as I understand it, none of them gets the least bit of attention — except the little girl. Maybe that's why — " she broke off, thoughtfully.

Mr. Sanders replied, with a good-natured smile, "P.T.A. gossip, probably." He had his coat on and was helping Joanie with hers.

"No, but they do say Mrs. Mason wanted a little

100

girl so badly that when she finally got one, she completely forgot she still had five boys to take care of," his wife explained, somewhat huffily.

"Yes, dear. Well, 'bye — we won't be long."

"I'll keep the coffee hot," Mrs. Sanders answered.

Once on the road, Joanie said, "Daddy, did you tell Mother where we are going? And where *are* we going, anyway?"

"I'm sure your mother knows we are going to the Masons' house."

"Oh," Joanie said, in some dismay. But a glance at her father seemed to reassure her and she went on, "I guess Mother meant Maxine. She's in Third. Maxine's absolutely repulsive, Daddy. Spoiled to death! No one likes her."

Surprised, Mr. Sanders murmured, "Really?" Then, after a few moments of contemplation, he added, "Perhaps your mother had the right idea. That just might be Tommy's problem — a spoiled sister. Certainly it could be the cause of his disliking girls. Since he would not be permitted to take his feeling out on Maxine, he would naturally find someone else. Your presence in his class gave him the chance he needed."

"*Needed*, Daddy?" Joanie looked puzzled, but after a moment she seemed to understand. "Oh, I see! You mean it isn't really me Tommy hates, it's Maxine! He only picks on me because he knows what he'd get for picking on his sister! Still — " This idea was of little comfort, her tone indicated.

"Where do the Masons live, Joanie?" Mr. Sanders asked, as they came to the main road where he must turn left or right.

101

"On Bluebell Lane. Don't you just love the names they give the roads here in Briarcliff Lake?" She was feeling slightly more cheerful. "But Daddy, why are we going there? I really don't want to."

"Oh, to settle a point," came the vague reply.

"You turn right on Grey Squirrel Drive," she told him, "and go past old Mr. Barker's place — he's a *character*, Daddy!"

"Yes?"

"The kids say he was a miner here just ages ago when they mined for gold. That's how old he is! He spoils squirrels and he keeps an absolutely fantastic mynah. Why, that bird says the most outrageous things!"

"How does he spoil squirrels?" Mr. Sanders asked, keeping the conversation away from Tommy for a while.

"He feeds them peanuts — all they can eat. Once, they broke into his house to get the nuts when he was away for a few weeks. They just about wrecked his place looking for that sack of peanuts. They dug into the upholstery and gnawed around the cupboards and had a marvelous time!" Joanie laughed as though she had seen the whole thing with her own eyes.

"That wasn't very sporting of the squirrels, considering Mr. Barker's kindness to them," Mr. Sanders commented, making the turn into Bluebell Lane.

With Tommy's home so near, Joanie lapsed into unhappy silence again and soon the car came to a stop before the Masons' front door.

Joanie wished it were lighter outdoors so her father might better see Tommy's home. It had been a huge barn at one time, she had been told, and it still retained the style of one. But someone with imagination — Mr.

102

Mason, perhaps? — had converted it into an attractive house big enough to accommodate a growing family. It did need paint, she remembered, but then the Masons were much more concerned about their horses and the stables which they owned and depended upon for their livelihood. Mr. Mason and the three older boys were kept very busy. Maybe they didn't have any time left for painting the house. Their stables on the main road certainly looked beautiful, all red and white, with BAR-M painted on a huge sign over the gate. Hundreds of people rented the Mason horses during the summer to ride the many trails near Briarcliff Lake.

Joanie began to tremble as her father pressed the button to ring the door bell. Fearfully, she wondered if the Masons knew she was to blame for Tommy's illness. They wouldn't be so ready to excuse her as her parents were.

From within the house came the loud blaring of a radio or TV. Joanie almost wished the door bell wouldn't be heard above the other noise. But at once the door was inched open by Maxine Mason who peered cautiously through the slight opening. She said, in a thin, piping voice, "What do you want? My mamma's busy — " She seemed ready to shut the door again.

"Good evening, young lady. I'm Mr. Sanders, the High School principal," Mr. Sanders made haste to introduce himself. At the same time, there was a slight note of authority in his voice which was meant to impress the little girl to the point of admitting them.

But Maxine didn't move, either to speak again or to open the door any wider. She just stared at them in a manner that could have been either insolent or only stupid. But then, from within the house, came a woman's voice. "Who is it, precious?" At that, Maxine opened the door a little wider and called back, "It's Ronnie's High School Principal on account of Ronnie must've done somethin' awful, Mamma. You want I should let him in?"

Joanie wondered if she herself had suddenly become invisible as she listened to her father say, severely, "Young lady —"

He was interrupted by Mrs. Mason's loud call, "Yes! Sure! You don't keep the *Principal* standing on the doorstep, for goodness' sakes! You come on in, Mr. Sanders!"

Maxine, apparently unperturbed by her mother's reply, opened the door wider again and permitted the two to enter. How sure of herself Maxine seemed, Joanie thought, unable to understand such behavior. So positive she could do no wrong! She was that way at school, too, strutting about the school grounds like a princess who didn't have to have consideration for anyone. All her fussy dresses and fancy hairdos and her turned-up nose! No wonder she was so unpopular.

Maxine led the way to the living room, dimly lighted because a TV program was in progress. Mrs. Mason came hurrying in, wiping her hands on her apron, full of apologies.

"Precious, will you go and dry the spoons for Mamma?" she said to Maxine with an adoring smile.

Maxine grimaced and said, "Aw, do I have to? Right now? Can't I just find out what Ronnie did?"

Trying to keep the irritation from his voice, Mr. Sanders said, "Ronnie hasn't done a thing out of line, to my knowledge. We came because of Tommy, Mrs. Mason. We wanted to know how he is getting along."

Maxine looked disappointed as her mother turned back to her to say, "There now, you see? So you can dry Mamma's spoons for her, after all. Please? Like a nice little girl?"

Maxine took a firm stance. Then she pulled in her lips and said with finality, "After. I will after Mr. Sanders goes."

Joanie was wondering what her own mother would say if she received a reply like this from her daughter. Certainly she would not smile in the resigned way Mrs. Mason was now doing!

To Mr. Sanders, Maxine's mother said, "You understand, having a little girl of your own, don't you, Mr. Sanders? They like to listen in."

Joanie resented being classed with Maxine, but she caught her father's warning glance and remained silent. A small dog trotted into the room and she occupied herself in patting him.

Mr. Sanders said, "We won't keep you, Mrs. Mason. You do seem to be busy. But how is Tommy?"

Primly, Mrs. Mason said, "Doing as well as can be expected."

"I'm sure he will soon be well again," Mr. Sanders replied reassuringly.

Maxine broke in. "It was his own fault. Going out at night in his bare feet! He's awful, Tommy is."

Mr. Sanders shot a swift glance at Joanie and said, simply, "Oh?" It was an invitation to Maxine to go on.

Mrs. Mason took it up from there. "Yes, I'm afraid he brought it on himself all right, though I shouldn't be condemning the poor boy while he's lying there suffering. He was sniffling something awful by breakfasttime. Sniffling and sneezing. I wanted him to stay home from school and ordinarily he'd have jumped at the chance. But he didn't want to miss any of the fun of the first snowfall. You know how boys are. So he went anyway, and by ten o'clock he was back home on account of the nurse saying he should be in bed. I guess he was glad to go, by the time he got home. To bed, I mean. My, what a fever!"

"I wouldn't do a thing like that," Maxine said, primly.

"No, precious, I'm sure you wouldn't." Mrs. Mason gave Mr. Sanders a weary smile and said, "I don't know what I'd do without the comfort of my little girl. Do you have any boys, Mr. Sanders? If you do, you know what I mean!"

"Well, yes, but he's still a baby," Mr. Sanders admitted.

Joanie was immediately on the defensive. Why did Daddy have to sound as though he was apologizing for having a son? Golly, she wouldn't trade Danny for Maxine! This was one time a boy didn't seem to be the worst thing that could happen to a family. Daddy was probably just being polite.

"Well, we won't take any more of your time, Mrs. Mason. We do hope Tommy is back in school before long and feeling fine." He glanced at Joanie. "And please tell him Joanie Sanders came by to inquire about him, will you?"

"Yes, indeed, sir. It was nice and thoughtful of you both to come. Well, that's a little girl for you — right?"

106

The woman bestowed a smile upon Joanie.

Once back in the car, Joanie exploded. "Oh!" was really all she said, but it expressed most of what she was feeling.

Her father laughed. "I must admit I've always rather liked little girls, but I never thought of them as saints before."

"Ugh! I feel like Pollyanna!"

"But you feel a lot better about Tommy?" her father asked.

"Oh, of course. Thanks, Daddy, for taking me there. How did you know?"

"One of the secrets fathers have," he teased.

Back home again, they found Mrs. Sanders in the living room waiting for them. There was a steaming pot of hot chocolate ready and a generous wedge of cake apiece. Joanie was suddenly ravenously hungry.

She swallowed the last of her chocolate and wiped cake crumbs from her mouth. Then she asked, "Do you think it would be all right for me to send some flowers to Tommy while he is in the hospital? I think I have enough money in my piggy bank to pay for them."

"Why, I think it would be a very nice thing to do," her mother replied, smiling and looking proud. Mr. Sanders nodded. He too seemed very pleased.

TEN

THANKSGIVING WEEK ARRIVED AND with it Tommy's return to school. Though he was not the most popular boy in his class, everyone showed genuine pleasure in his recovery. He looked pale and not too strong, but he insisted he was feeling fine; and anyway, he declared, he had to be back in time because his part as the Wicked Queen was so important to the play.

Joanie suggested, "Besides, the Wicked Queen is *supposed* to have a white face, isn't she, Miss Coles? All wicked people seem to have white faces in story books. All Tommy will need is eyebrow stuff and maybe a false nose — the kind with a hook."

Furtively, so that no one else could see, Tommy gave Joanie a smile. The smile as good as told her that his teasing and meanness were things of the past, so far as she was concerned. Surprised, she thought, "Why, I'll miss the teasing!" And then Joanie wondered why she should feel this way.

Right now, however, the big thing was the play. Joanie nagged all the boys toward perfection in their individual performances and practised her own part unceasingly. The Fourth Grade simply had to win! Not only that, she had discovered that she loved to act. Nothing short of perfection satisfied her. She was quick to memorize and her naturally expressive way of speaking and reading no longer gave the boys cause for laughter. Now, they freely admitted, they were counting on Joanie most of all.

Miss Coles asked, "How is your mother getting along with the costumes, Joanie? I understand she is helping some of the other mothers, too."

"Well, in a way," Joanie replied. "But suggesting, mainly. They didn't know just what to do about the dwarfs' costumes till Mother suggested they might dye extra-large T shirts woodsy colors. They will be worn over sloppy-fitting pants loaned by fathers and older brothers. Oh, I don't mean the pants fit the fathers and brothers sloppily," she giggled.

The children laughed along with Joanie and Miss Coles, and Tommy said, "Well, *my* father's pants fit him sloppy! Not his dress-up ones, but the ones he wears around the stables. A good thing I'm not a dwarf in the play on account of my father's almost a giant and I guess I'd just about get lost in a pair of his old pants!"

More laughter greeted his remark. When there was quiet again, Joanie went on with enthusiasm, "I've been helping, too. Mother and I have made shoes of felt — dark green, with long, pointed toes. The dwarfs' caps will be the tops of old nylon stockings dyed to match the T shirts. You'll love them!"

Joanie's own costumes were something she was saving as a surprise. She knew they were the most beautiful in the world! She had tried them on a dozen times and now they hung ready in her room. Puffy sleeves, velvet bodices, full skirts of pastel-colored organdy over crinoline petticoats. She almost wished these were the days when little girls dressed in such clothes all the time, forgetting an earlier desire to wear blue jeans.

The night before the performance Mrs. Sanders put Joanie's hair up in large, fat rollers, copying the Snow White hair style from the story book. Joanie was sure she wouldn't be able to sleep — and not entirely on account of the rollers. Even on a feather mattress and a pillow of clouds, sleep would be impossible. Or so she thought. Yet suddenly it was morning!

She rubbed her eyes, jumped out of bed before her mother had time to call her, and hurried into her school clothes.

At breakfast she told her parents, "Archie's father had Archie's costume made to order by a costumer in the city. I can hardly wait to see it!" She accepted a biscuit absently. "Daddy, do you think you will be able to come?" she asked, her big eyes imploring.

"Oh, I think I might be able to sneak off for an hour," he smiled back, then admitted that he wouldn't miss the performance for the world. "My daughter's stage debut? I should say not!" He tweaked Joanie's small nose affectionately.

"Stop that, Daddy — I mustn't have a red nose!" she laughed, excited and happy.

The morning went by somehow, with no one caring one whit about whether the Pilgrims landed on Plymouth Rock in 1620 or 1950! Such matters could wait — today it was the play! Miss Coles was very understanding and criticized no one.

As it turned out, however, they were not permitted

to forget about the Pilgrims entirely. The play presented by the Third Graders that afternoon concerned the very first Thanksgiving, which of course had everything to do with the Pilgrims. It was a very good presentation and earned loud and prolonged applause.

This did not dampen the spirits of the Fourth Graders, however. They were all perfectly confident that their own play could not be excelled. They joined generously in the applause, demonstrating their good sportsmanship.

Then their own big moment arrived. With the curtains closed on the final act of the Third Graders' play, and the P.T.A. president on stage giving a brief talk, the set was made ready for *Snow White and the Seven Dwarfs*. There was much subdued laughter backstage as the boys viewed each other in costume. Comments flew back and forth.

"Hey, Damon, there's no glass in your specs!"

"Gosh, look at Bobby! How Dopey can a guy look!"

"Aw, look at yourself — your cap's on backwards!"

Their fun helped to dispel the nervousness that usually precedes a performance. Then the boys began to notice Joanie, though she pretended not to be aware of it. Being boys, she didn't expect lavish compliments. Still, she could see in their eyes their surprise and admiration. It was almost as though most of them were looking at her for the first time. Archie, never one to hesitate in expressing his real feelings, said, "You look awfully pretty, Joanie."

"Yeah," Jack agreed, then busied himself with a shoelace.

It was enough. More than she had expected, really.

She stood back to survey Archie in his custom-made outfit and was astonished that a boy could look beautiful.

"Well, la-de-daw! If it isn't Queen Sourpuss herself!" someone exclaimed, snickering, as Tommy appeared in his lavish costume. He walked very stiffly and self-consciously and made a hideous face at his tormentor.

And then they were called to order, for the curtain was about to rise. Faces became immobile as each player took his place and stood in breathless silence, waiting. On stage, the lights enhancing her loveliness, stood Joanie, alone except for Tommy Mason poised in the wings, ready to enter.

Everything went off beautifully, with the exception, perhaps, of Tommy falling flat on his face once when he tripped over the long train of his costume. But he scrambled to his feet, unruffled, and the good-natured audience hardly giggled at all. Joanie felt sure that the few who did express their amusement were known to Tommy and would be settled with later.

Joanie herself sailed through her part like a seasoned trouper. Her one uneasy moment came when Archie, as Prince Charming, came on stage astride an elongated hobby horse to claim her for his bride. All through rehearsals Miss Coles had said it was not actually necessary for Archie to kiss Joanie. But she added that if he should choose to do so when the play was performed before an audience, it would add realism. So Joanie waited and wondered. When Archie came on, poised and superbly confident, she knew he intended to perform in the best stage tradition.

She was grateful indeed for the curtain. It started

to descend at the very moment Archie's lips touched her rosy cheek. In her confusion, she failed to hear the tumultuous applause until, suddenly, up went the curtain and she was urged by Miss Coles to take a bow. "And hold Archie's hand as you do so," the teacher whispered.

None knew how Joanie's heart pounded as she took her bows. All the audience saw was a lovely princess with her fairy prince, acknowledging well-deserved praise.

When Joanie found her parents later, standing by the refreshment table, she was surprised to see that her mother's eyes were moist with tears.

"I'm just so proud of you, darling!" was her mother's apologetic explanation as she planted a kiss on Joanie's cheek.

Somehow her mother's kiss served to erase the one Archie had placed there only a few minutes earlier. It made it easier for her to face him again. She saw that Mr. Sanders was engaged in conversation with Archie's father, the Professor, and so it was only natural that Archie should join the group too.

Unabashed, Archie said, "I think we did very well, don't you, Joanie? My father thinks so too."

"Oh, yes. But we won't know about the prize until the Christmas party," Joanie sighed, feeling quite at ease now. "Anyway, even if we don't win, I think it was a lovely play and it was so much fun doing it."

"Spoken like a trouper," Archie's father said, adding, "I certainly wouldn't want to be a judge in a thing like this!"

"Nor I," Mr. Sanders agreed fervently.

"The judges are over there," Archie said, pointing

to a small group of people standing near the door. "Doctor Smith, the dentist, Mr. Collier, who owns the feed store, and Mrs. Alsop. She plays the organ at the Community Church and lives alone. None of them have any children in our school so no one can accuse them of playing favorites."

Everyone began to leave the auditorium. Joanie found herself paired off with Archie as their parents started on foot down the road.

Archie asked, "Would you like to see my fish, Joanie?"

"Fish? Don't tell me you found time to go fishing this morning!" Joanie exclaimed with a light-hearted laugh.

"Oh no," he answered, seriously. "It's off season for fishing, you know. I mean my collection. I have some very rare specimens — it's a sort of hobby."

Joanie called to her parents to ask permission. Then, when it came time to turn off at Lakeshore Drive, she turned with Archie. "I can only stay a little while," she told him. "We have dinner quite early."

At that moment Jack and Bobby whizzed by on bicycles and Jack yelled, "Joanie has a boy friend! Joanie has a boy friend!" Bobby took up the chant and added, "Archie loves Joanie! Archie loves Joanie!"

Joanie blushed. So did Archie. Then Joanie said, with a toss of her head which caused her curls to bob up and down, "Boys! You see what I mean? Never happy unless they're acting up. I can't stand them, can you?" Then she laughed at Archie's dismay. "Oh! Oh, I didn't mean you!" she added, chagrined.

"Look — I *had* to kiss you," Archie replied, looking

miserable as he stared after the disappearing cyclists. "I m-mean, it was just to add realism — as Miss Coles said — "

Joanie asked, "You mean you don't really like me?"

"Joanie, I didn't say that. Sure I like you. I mean, well — I'm taking you to see my fish, aren't I?" As though that were proof positive.

The fish, as Joanie admitted a few moments later, were something to be proud of. She was amazed when she saw them. They were in a fabulous tank which was set into a long, panelled wall. Soft lighting played on the colorful tropical specimens. Lovely water plants and oddly shaped rocks, resembling small castles, gave the tank a look of fairyland. Joanie watched, fascinated, as the fish moved about. Archie knew the name of every specimen in the tank and pointed out his favorites with great pride.

"It's beautiful, Archie. I had no idea! I thought you were going to show me a little bowlful of goldfish. This — well, it's almost like going to a real aquarium. I went to one once when we were on vacation in San Francisco."

"Fish are my hobby," Archie said again, pleased that Joanie was so impressed.

For a while longer, Joanie gazed in fascinated admiration. Then Archie's father came in and she said she really must be going. She thanked Archie for showing her the fish and said good-bye.

As Joanie walked toward home, she was thinking not of the fish nor of the play. She thought how sad it was that Archie had no mother waiting to greet him when he came home from school as she had. His house seemed so cold, somehow, in spite of the beautiful fish tank and the big, comfortable leather chairs in the living room. She knew that warmth in a house meant more than a thermostat on the wall and logs in the fireplace. It meant the sound of someone singing in the kitchen and a glass of milk with some cookies waiting for you on the table. Until today she had taken such things for granted.

By the time she arrived home, Joanie was feeling quite depressed on Archie's account, which probably would have surprised Archie himself. She opened the door and found her own mother in the living room, taking off Danny's outdoor things. Danny had spent the afternoon at the baby sitter's. He looked the picture of contentment on his mother's lap. Joanie's heart suddenly filled with joy at the sight and she flung her arms around her mother's neck almost fiercely. "Oh, I love you, Mother! I love you!" she cried, as she felt the tears sting her eyelids.

ELEVEN

WITH THE WINTER SEASON came several snowfalls that inspired sports-minded city dwellers to desert temporarily their palm trees and lawns and colorful flower beds. The ski runs and tows were in full operation at Briarcliff Lake and the ice skating rink was doing an excellent business. Permanent residents were delighted at the early-season prosperity and gladly worked hard to keep the pleasure-seekers happy.

One day Joanie came home from school to say, wistfully, "I wish I was a boy — "

Astonished, her father could only stare. Mrs. Sanders looked up from her magazine to exclaim, "For heaven's sake, don't you feel well, Joanie?"

"I feel fine. And I mean it. I wish I was a boy." She sounded almost disconsolate.

Mr. Sanders found his tongue and said to his wife, "Well, that's a switch!" Then, turning to Joanie, "Why? So you can hate yourself?" For Joanie had still persisted in her avowed dislike of boys, in spite of several recent occurrences to the contrary.

In an injured tone, Joanie said, "Of course not. I mean, I wish I was a boy in one respect only."

"You like the way they do their hair," her father guessed, his eyes laughing at her.

"Don't be silly. No. It's just that all the boys get to go into the forest to chop down Christmas trees. Oh, Daddy, don't you think that's the most wonderful thing anyone could do — cut down a Christmas tree?" She became dreamy-eyed.

"It sounds like fun," Mr. Sanders conceded, then added, "However, I was under the impression that no one is allowed to cut down trees in this vicinity. This is a national forest — it belongs to everyone in the nation. If one group is permitted to help itself to Christmas trees, just imagine what it would be like if everyone else insisted on the same privilege."

"Well, there wouldn't be any forest fires," Joanie grinned, feeling quite clever.

"Or any watersheds to prevent floods," her father was quick to retort in a serious voice.

"Anyway, it is all right for the boys to do it. The forestry men are going along with them to tell them which trees they may chop down. Actually, they'll be helping tidy up the forest, Miss Coles says. And then, the school is to have a Christmas tree sale and a wreath and ornament sale to raise money for the school library. We need new books."

"What an excellent idea!" Mrs. Sanders said.

"So that's why I wish I was a boy," Joanie continued.

"And after all the trees were cut, what would you do? Wish you were a girl again? Honestly!" Mr. Sanders shook his head in a manner which said, "I give up!"

Joanie sounded a little petulant as she went on, "But to cut down your own tree! All the girls get to do

is collect and paint pine cones and acorns and euca-
lyptus pods. At least, that's all the Third and Fourth
graders are to do. The bigger girls in the Seventh and
Eighth grades will make della Robia wreaths from the
things we paint. They will be beautiful — Mrs. Westcott
showed us a sample. You will buy one, won't you,
Mother? I can take your order right now."

Joanie paused for breath, then continued enthusiastically. "And we are to draw names in our class so
we can each buy a little gift for someone else in the
class, for the Christmas party!" She paused again, looking thoughtful, then added, "I wonder who will choose
my name? Oh, isn't Christmas fun, though! Still — I do
wish I could chop down a tree!"

Her father groaned and her mother shook her head
in mock despair, saying, "Honestly!" as she rose from
her chair. "Well, I'm afraid I'm a little late getting dinner started, all this has been so interesting. Joanie, how
about a little help?" She smiled at Joanie and led the
way to the kitchen.

Joanie was given the task of tearing up lettuce for
the salad while her mother trimmed fat from the lamb
chops. "Would you like to go to the city with me on
Saturday, Joanie?" Mrs. Sanders asked, slipping the
chops under the broiler. "Christmas shopping?"

"Oh, yes!" Tree-chopping was momentarily forgotten.

"I would like to buy you a doll," Mrs. Sanders said
hesitantly, her eyes intent upon her task.

"A doll? For Christmas? B-but why tell me *now*?
Is it because I'm big enough to know? Mother, I love
surprises!" Joanie sounded a little disappointed, though

she tried not to.

"Well, dear, not exactly. You see, Danny broke your best doll this morning and I want to replace it. I'm sorry it happened and I do hope we can find one just like it."

Joanie's first reaction was one of annoyance with Danny. Then, because she was in an unusually happy mood and the prospect of a Christmas shopping tour was so exciting, she laughed and said, "Well, after all, he *is* a boy. He wouldn't have any respect for a doll, I suppose."

"I seem to remember that you broke a compass of your daddy's when you were about the same age as Danny," Mrs. Sanders remarked.

Joanie smiled ruefully. "Anyway, I don't really need a doll right now," she said. "I ought to have a few more things not quite so — so — " She fumbled for the right word.

"Childish?" suggested her mother.

"Well, not exactly. I do still like dolls, but — well — a doll *is* terribly girlish, isn't it?" She hoped her Mother wouldn't get the wrong impression from all this. It didn't mean that boys were suddenly becoming more tolerable to her just because she had a chemistry set in mind. Certainly not! Still, a girl who owned a chemistry set was likely to arouse their respect, she thought.

She wandered across the kitchen to glance out of the window, the lettuce momentarily forgotten. "I was thinking about a chemistry set," she said, casually. Then she saw the Woodleys' beautiful big collie go scampering by and another idea struck her. "Mother! Wouldn't it be lovely for us to have a dog? For me to get a puppy for Christmas?"

Mrs. Sanders was eyeing Danny who was pounding on the tray of his high chair with a spoon. She said, "Well — I don't know, Joanie. We had thought it might be nice to have a dog up here, but we rather wanted to wait until Danny could be counted on not to mistreat it. He's so young yet."

"Oh," Joanie replied confidently, "if there's one thing good about boys, it's that they really love dogs, Mother. Why, even Tommy Mason."

"I know. But babies don't realize that when they pull a puppy's tail, it hurts. However, I'll talk it over with your father. If we should decide it's all right for you to have one, what kind would you like?"

Joanie didn't hesitate for long. The dog had to be a large one. She loved little poodles, of course, but a poodle wouldn't impress the boys very much. Besides, a poodle belonged in town, somehow, she thought. She said, her eyes shining, "Well, since we live in the mountains and have all this snow, I think there is only one kind of dog to have, don't you? The kind that can pull sleds and rescue lost people — and everything!"

Mrs. Sanders gulped. "Don't tell me! Let me guess. Could it be that you mean a Saint Bernard?" She looked as if she hoped she were wrong.

"Oh, I know what you're thinking, Mother. But look at it this way. If I had a horse — well, no dog would eat as much as a horse, would he? And lots of the kids have horses — "

"What's this about horses and how much they eat?" asked Mr. Sanders, who had just entered the kitchen. Then he grinned and added, "Right now, I'm so hungry I could beat any horse at eating."

122

"Dinner will be on the table very soon, dear," his wife reassured him and then went on to explain, "Joanie apparently does not believe that the best gifts come in small packages." She pulled out the broiler and transferred the chops to a platter. "How about setting the table — the chops won't stay hot, you know. Goodness, I'm doing everything topsy-turvy — do please hurry."

Joanie took out the tablecloth and commented, "When I get my Christmas present, we won't have to worry about what to do with cold lamb chops."

"At the risk of sounding stupid, I can't seem to make head or tail of what you are talking about," Mr. Sanders remarked, placing knives and forks on the table.

Mrs. Sanders said, "Joanie, you haven't been promised that particular present, yet. I told you, your father and I have to discuss it first. As for a Saint Bernard — !"

"Ah-ha!" Mr. Sanders grinned, understanding at last.

Danny, meanwhile, was pounding harder than ever, demanding both food and attention. Dinner proceeded without further discussion regarding Christmas gifts.

When they drew names for gift-giving at school, Joanie came up with Jack's. She wondered, naturally, who had drawn hers. She didn't really expect a boy to show much interest in the selection of a gift for a girl and said as much at home that evening.

"He'll probably go out and buy a bag of marbles," she told her parents.

"Whatever you receive, Joanie, I hope you will be gracious enough to accept it with gratitude," said her father.

"Gracious! Gratitude! After all, I don't expect a diamond crown, Daddy!" she exclaimed, affecting great amusement. "But I do know my manners, after all. But you must admit it's a lot easier to say you love something if you actually do."

"Oh, for goodness' sake, you don't have to go overboard. There are many tactful things you can find to say if the gift seems — er — unusual," he smiled.

"Like, 'Oh Eric, you shouldn't have! Honestly, it's just too much!'?" Joanie grinned.

"Something like that," her father sighed.

"Only I won't say 'Eric', because I won't know who — "

"If I might change the subject, Joanie," her mother said, "how are the grades coming along? You haven't talked about much else but the play lately, and if you are planning to leave Fourth Grade next month they should be a matter of concern to you."

"Oh, don't worry, Mother," came Joanie's airy reply. "I'm quite sure I'll make it. Wait till I bring home my report card — you'll be absolutely amazed."

"H'm. I certainly hope so," Mr. Sanders commented. "Promotion or no, if the boys can cause you to jump from a C-minus to a B-plus in one semester, my hat is off to them."

"And if it's a plain and simple A?" Joanie asked.

"Then hats off to you too."

Smugly, Joanie returned to the book she had been reading. Before starting to read again, however, she asked, "Daddy, what can I give Jack? I don't know what a boy would like."

Her father laughed. "Ha! A few minutes ago you

worried that a certain boy wouldn't know what to buy for you. Isn't it obvious now that he will ask his mother for suggestions, just as you have asked me in the case of Jack?"

Of course. Unless it happened to be Archie. She opened her book and began to read.

Joanie eagerly awaited the day of the Christmas party at school. It seemed as though it would never come. With each successive day excitement grew, not only for Joanie but for all the children. There were to be parties in every room and, as a grand climax, the winning play was to be announced. Even though the Fourth Graders felt confident their play had been the best, they had to concede that perhaps the judges might have another opinion. This uncertainty added to the tension.

At last the day arrived. All the boys were shiny-clean, dressed in their best shirts and slacks, shoes polished and hair slickly combed. Joanie, wearing her red velvet jumper with the white taffeta blouse, felt very Christmasy. Even Miss Coles was all dressed up in a dress made of some pretty green woolen material. When she saw Joanie she laughed and said, "Together, we'd make a fine Christmas tree, Joanie!" Her comment set the pace for a gay party.

Mrs. Riley, the P.T.A. room mother for Fourth Grade, was putting out brightly colored candy and cookies and napkins on the long tressled table against the wall.

"We'll have a few games first," Miss Coles told the children. "Mrs. Riley brought the donkey tail game and I think that would be a good one to start off with."

Fifteen or twenty minutes of hilarity with the donkey tails was followed by one or two guessing games and a game called "Where's Mr. Peter's Cat?" A bean bag served as the "cat" and it was Joanie who found it, right in the center of the basket containing the gifts. Surely a place no one else even thought to look, but Joanie considered a basket a fitting place for a cat to sit! She didn't have to rummage, of course; it was right on top of the presents, in full view. But as she reached for it she had time to see her own name tagged to an interesting looking package. Who could be the donor? And had his mother wrapped it? Would a boy choose such pretty ribbon?

With the games over, someone asked, "When do the presents get given out, Miss Coles?"

"First, we will have the treats — Mrs. Riley says the ice cream is getting a little soft," Miss Coles replied.

This seemed to satisfy the boys and, when Joanie saw the plates, she was also willing to postpone the gift-giving portion of the party. The ice cream was in the form of small Santa heads, while tiny cupcakes were decorated to resemble Christmas tree ornaments. Pink lemonade was available as a thirst quencher.

There was an identical, gift-wrapped package for each pupil, each bearing a tag which read, "A Very Merry Christmas to you, from Mary Coles!"

Soon there was a happy chorus of "Thank you, Miss Coles!" as these gift packages were opened. The teacher had presented each of her ten pupils with a small box of thank-you notes, most certain to prove useful after Christmas Day.

The refreshments having been enjoyably disposed

126

of, Miss Coles began handing out the gifts. "Tommy Mason — ," "Eric Roberts — ," "Jack Dawson — "

Joanie caught her breath. Would Jack like the book? She had selected *Robinson Crusoe* at her father's suggestion. She didn't have time, just then, to watch Jack open his package, for her own name was being called. She stepped forward to receive her gift.

Her fingers shook as she untied the ribbon. She hoped she wasn't being watched by the boys. Suddenly she gasped. On its bed of snowy cotton in the opened box glowed a tiny enameled heart attached to a fine, gold-colored chain. The heart bore her own initial. There was, after all, no need to pretend! The problem was how to express herself adequately! She had never dreamed — ! Oh, who could *he* be? So she could thank just the right boy? She didn't want to say, to a roomful of boys, "Oh, it's absolutely beautiful!"

Yet she had no other choice. Finally, lifting her eyes from the gift, she saw that the eyes of all the others were upon her and the little box she held. She realized that the whole class must be wondering, even as she herself was wondering, who could have given her such a lovely gift. Knowing nods, sly little grins, furtive glances at one another, and yet no one really knew. Except *the one*, Joanie thought, her face reddening uncomfortably. She didn't dare look at any one boy in particular. Yet she ached to know!

"Whoever gave me *Robinson Crusoe*, thanks!" Jack said suddenly, thus starting a series of similar expressions of appreciation from the others. Joanie almost forgot herself and started to say "You're welcome," but caught herself in time.

And then Miss Coles was handing another package to Joanie, saying in some surprise, "Well, my goodness, here are two more gifts for you, Joanie!"

"Oh! B-but there must be some mistake," Joanie protested.

"See for yourself," Miss Coles suggested, showing Joanie that the tags were clearly marked with her name.

Joanie accepted the packages and, feeling herself the center of attention, opened them with some embarrassment. There were two very pretty handkerchiefs in one, and in the other a small bottle of perfume. She felt somehow very humble and almost ready to cry.

Then suddenly Miss Coles clapped her hands for attention and said they had better start tidying up the room, that there remained only five more minutes before they were to file into the auditorium to hear which grade had won the prize for its play. She made no further attempt to keep order; excitement had now reached its peak and there was no controlling it.

Surprisingly, Damon asked Joanie, "You won't cry,

will you Joanie, if we don't win?"

"Of course I won't," Joanie answered, moved by his concern.

"Well, I only meant you were so pretty. You were a wonderful Snow White." Damon, usually so quiet and indifferent, now seemed as eager as the rest to hear the results of the contest.

But even Chris and Mark, who usually ignored Joanie completely, now agreed with Damon. Said Mark, "Yes, Joanie was good all right, wasn't she, Chris?"

His twin nodded. "Even if the rest of us don't win, Joanie should," he said, generously.

Unable to believe in "instant change," Joanie decided it must be the Christmas spirit which filled the boys with all this good will toward her.

At last all the pupils were assembled in the auditorium, the noise and scuffling silenced. Mrs. Polson, the P.T.A. president, was presented by the principal, just as though none of those in the room had ever met her before.

"As you all know, the play contest idea originated with our wonderful P.T.A., and even though it did not provide the prize, it was due to the efforts of P.T.A. members that the Chamber of Commerce was prevailed upon to do so. So I think this is a good time to show all our parents and teachers who belong to the P.T.A. just how much we appreciate the many fine things they do for us throughout the year."

Everyone applauded. Vociferous cheers came from some of the boys and others stamped their feet enthusiastically. At last the audience was subdued and Mrs. Polson rose to speak. There was suddenly such a silence one could almost hear her smile! The big moment was here at last! To Joanie, it was like a sweet pain, almost better than knowing. For supposing — but she refused to think beyond this moment.

"Well, my dear young people," Mrs. Polson began. "I know how excited you all must be. You have had parties and received gifts and had a wonderful day. I know, too, how much you all want to go home now to prepare for the holidays still to come. So I will not bore you with a long speech. I do want to take time, however, to pass along another piece of good news to you. It concerns the sale of the Christmas trees and the lovely della Robia wreaths which decorate so many doors in Briarcliff Lake this season."

Oh dear, thought Joanie, can't she get to the point? A sidelong glance told her the boys were feeling the same way, that at this moment they couldn't care less about the sale or how nice the wreaths looked!

"I had a phone call this morning," Mrs. Polson continued, "from Mr. Carter, the President of the bank. He said that if you boys and girls had raised over a hundred dollars from the sale he would match the amount, dollar for dollar. I was very happy to be able to tell him that the amount realized on the sale was one hundred and sixty-five dollars! So, with Mr. Carter's most generous contribution, there is a sum of three hundred and thirty dollars available for new library books! That means a lot of marvelous reading for all of you for a long time to come — "

Mrs. Polson paused deliberately, waiting for the applause due both Mr. Carter and the entire success of the sale. Although the children were indeed very pleased,

130

their applause was less prolonged than it had been previously, and soon Mrs. Polson was able to go on.

"Now, on to the contest!" she smiled. "The judges have asked me to tell you how very, very difficult it was for them to select a winner. They feel that every grade in the school did an outstanding job and, because of that, each grade is going to receive a special award — a lovely framed picture to hang on its classroom wall. The pictures also are to be donated by our very generous Chamber of Commerce."

Loud applause greeted this announcement. Then, raising a hand for silence, Mrs. Polson went on, "But now for the *big* announcement! The prize for the best presentation goes to — " She paused, giving her audience a tantalizing smile. Could it be, Joanie wondered, that Mrs. Polson was reluctant at this final moment to disappoint those who, inevitably, must be disappointed? One prize, eight plays! A hundred hopeful hearts!

Then Mrs. Polson's face assumed a seriousness as she went on, "The prize goes to the grade that gave a play depicting one of the earliest Christmases on record — a play which points up the true spirit which should always be present at Christmastime. Perhaps this is the reason the prize has been awarded to this particular grade — the play was seasonal without being of the usual holiday variety. But, of course, the judging was also based on the performance and the performers."

Oh, dear, thought Joanie, desperately, won't she ever — ! Even so, it can't be us — it can't be us — Her heart began sinking slowly as the implication of Mrs. Polson's words seeped in. A Christmas play. A *Christmas* play, she'd said.

131

"And so, without further delay, I now declare the winning grade to be — Mrs. Harriod's Eighth Grade! Congratulations to each and every one of you!" Beaming, Mrs. Polson sat down.

There was a moment when no one spoke or moved. Some faces twitched, others looked blank. Still others looked stunned. The sudden rustling and spontaneous whooping which came a few seconds later definitely originated from the rear of the auditorium where the Eighth Grade pupils sat. Or had been sitting, for now they rose as one and their lusty voices joined in joyous sounds of victory.

Then, one by one, other grades joined in. Good sportsmanship must prevail. There could, after all, be only one winner. That had been known from the start. Soon the applause for the Eighth Grade was deafening and the teachers' faces all seemed to relax. Smiles were everywhere.

Presently the teachers were urging the children to be seated again. Mrs. Westcott was standing with hand uplifted, pleading for silence.

"Just a few minutes more, children, and then you will be dismissed. Mrs. Polson has one more announcement to make, so if you will give her your attention — " The principal smiled at the P.T.A. president, who once again took the center of the stage.

She said, "You see, the judges felt it was hardly a fair competition — " A number of pupils exchanged glances which said they heartily agreed. Mrs. Polson continued, "Since the ages of the contestants covered such a wide range, it was decided to give a duplicate prize to the younger age group. I am indeed very happy

132

to tell you that the prize for this group was awarded, by unanimous vote, to the grade which gave that most delightful performance of *Snow White and the Seven Dwarfs*. Congratulations to each and every member of Miss Coles' Fourth Grade!"

Incredulous joy swept through the hearts of nine boys and one little girl. Pandemonium broke loose. There were whoops and cheers from all sides, exclamations of agreement such as were not heard following the first prize announcement. It was perfectly obvious that, had the choice been up to the school children themselves, *Snow White* would have won without debate.

Laughter and tears mingled without shame in Joanie's eyes and she smiled gently when Damon said in awe, "Gosh, Joanie, I expected you to cry for *not* winning! What are you crying for *now?*" Then, under his breath, he murmured in some perplexity, "Girls are awful funny — "

Quickly, however, Joanie blinked away the tears and rubbed her cheeks dry with her fists. Then she muttered, her face turned away from Damon, "I guess I must have something in my eye — " Vaguely, as from a distance, she heard Mrs. Westcott dismiss them all.

TWELVE

WHEN JOANIE ARRIVED HOME, exuberant with her good news, she found her grandparents had arrived for the holidays. Her greeting left something to be desired, for she could not wait to tell about the prize. With her grandmother's kiss still warm upon her cheek, Joanie said, "We won, Mother! We won!"

"Darling, how perfectly marvelous! But of course I knew you would — " her mother exulted. Then she turned to explain to the grandparents what it was all about. They seemed to be just as pleased and as proud of Joanie as was her mother.

"What part did you play, dear?" Grandmother asked.

"I had no choice," Joanie replied, making a face.

"She's the only girl in her class," Mrs. Sanders explained.

"Oh my! Oh, how difficult for you, dear!" Grandmother sounded sympathetic but hastened to add, "But of course it left you with the leading role, didn't it? So I suppose it's an ill wind — "

Grandfather interrupted to say, jovially, "Now we don't *know* that Joanie minds the boys, do we, Martha?"

134

"Well, all I know is, when I was Joanie's age it wouldn't have spelled bliss for *me!*" Grandmother retorted, laughing. "Do they tease you terribly, Joanie?"

"Tease!" Joanie replied, eloquently.

"Then you haven't a thing to worry about," Grandfather concluded. "When the boys stop teasing, then you have a problem."

"Why?" Joanie asked, somewhat puzzled.

Grandfather chuckled and pinched her cheek lightly. "Oh, it's their way of showing they like you," he said.

This was a most disconcerting idea! "Honestly?" Joanie asked, her eyes wide in surprise.

"You bet. I was a little boy myself once, you know." Grandfather's eyes twinkled.

Joanie slipped a hand into her pocket and her fingers felt the three little packages she had placed there. Was Grandfather right? The gifts certainly seemed to indicate as much, though she hadn't really thought of them that way. She had been so embarrassed that there hadn't been room for any other thoughts at the time. Now she wondered if she should have been very proud, secure in the knowledge that at least three of the boys liked her enough to buy her presents. Well, two, really, since one of them had no choice. Oh, but there were more than two! Archie surely liked her. And Damon. And —

She withdrew the packages from her pocket and shyly told her mother and her grandparents where they had come from.

"There now, doesn't that just prove what I told you?" Grandfather gave her a brief hug. It was difficult to tell if he was just teasing.

Joanie laughed, however, and said, "Anyway, I like grown-up boys quite well — " and kissed the top of his balding head.

After showing the contents of the packages, Joanie said, a little self-consciously, "Of course, I don't really *know*, but Archie's face was awfully red when Miss Coles gave me the gift package with the heart in it. But then it was quite warm in the room, so maybe it was just that."

"How about the other gifts?" her mother asked, seemingly very much interested in solving the mysteries.

"I — I really have no idea, Mother," Joanie confessed.

"I should think it was almost as much fun not knowing," Grandmother said.

Oh, but the heart! Joanie felt she had to know about that! She was alarmed, therefore, when, upon his return home, her father announced, "I invited Doctor Polster and his boy over for Christmas dinner."

Joanie interrupted with an impulsive, "Oh, Daddy, no!"

Everyone looked at her in surprise. It wasn't, she told herself unhappily, that she didn't want them, exactly. But how could she explain? There was no mother at Archie's house and she thought it had been very kind of her father to think of inviting the two to share the Sanders' festivities. But oh, if the other boys ever found out! They had teased her enough already about Archie, ever since the incident of the kiss at the end of the play. It didn't matter to them that Archie hadn't meant it, of course. And now, what with the heart and everything —

well, he simply couldn't come to dinner!

She became aware of the suggestion of contempt in her father's face and it shook her considerably. She started to remonstrate but he said, ignoring her, "Such incredible self-centeredness! What *is* it with you, Joanie?"

"Daddy, I — "

"But you needn't worry. Archie won't be here. The Professor said they had already accepted an invitation to the home of friends down the hill. They are to stay with them for a couple of days so I'm sure the boy will have a merry Christmas." He sounded almost sad as he turned away from her. Joanie had never felt so small in all her life.

By the following day, Mr. Sanders appeared to have forgotten the incident. Joanie, however, was finding it more difficult to do so. She felt ashamed and yet she was relieved that Archie wasn't coming. Upon reflection, she was inclined to place some of the blame upon the boys. If they hadn't teased her so much she would never have objected to Archie's coming to dinner, she argued with herself.

But this was Christmas Eve. She put aside any pointless worrying; this was no time to be glum! So many exciting things to do — Christmas Eve was almost more fun than Christmas Day! The tree had to be trimmed. Grandfather still loved to help with this chore and Mr. and Mrs. Sanders always humored him by waiting for his arrival.

Immediately after breakfast was over, Grandfather and Joanie were sent to the living room to begin the joyful task. It was a beautiful tree, even though Joanie

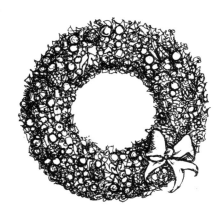

had not had the pleasure of chopping it down herself. Its pungent scent filled the entire house and Grandfather sniffed the air with satisfaction. He was like a little boy, Joanie thought, watching him go through the tree ornaments eagerly. Every once in a while he would hold one up for her to look at and would tell her a reminiscent tale about it: the angel, bought in the Mexican quarter in Los Angeles and now somewhat the worse for wear; a bluebird Daddy had bought, long before he ever became a daddy.

And so the morning went. Finished at last, the tree was a sparkling masterpiece and Joanie dimpled with pleasure when the grown-ups complimented her on such a fine job. Grandfather insisted he had spent more time watching than doing. She was inclined to agree! But he'd had a good time, she knew, and it had been nice of her parents to wait for him.

Off in a corner, Danny was discovered attempting to eat an artificial snowball. In the kitchen, Grandmother and Mrs. Sanders were making mince pies; from the radio came strains of Christmas music; with it all, Joanie was moved to deep emotion. Oh, there was nothing, but *nothing*, quite as wonderful as Christmas. To complete the picture, during the late afternoon a gentle snow began to fall and Mr. Sanders laid a log fire in the huge fireplace.

Later, Mrs. Sanders served a quick, easy dinner and then they all went to the candlelight service at the church. Walking down the aisle with the others, in the eerie light of a hundred wavering candles, Joanie somehow felt she was forgiven for whatever she might have said to hurt anyone. She made a silent promise to try being nicer in the future.

This gentle feeling remained with her long after the service was over. It warmed her as the family drove through the starlit night toward home. Everything looked fantastically beautiful to her as she gazed dreamily out of the car window. The new snow looked like the frosting on Mother's sugarplum cake! She yawned luxuriously. The lighted trees in the windows of homes along the way seemed to wink and twinkle cheery greetings to her. The scene was so story-bookish and delightful that she could all but hear the bells on Santa's sleigh and see his reindeer flashing their way through the sky.

Suddenly Daddy's voice reached her as through a haze. "Hey, sleepyhead! We're home! Come on, you have a stocking to hang and — "

Joanie started. Why, she had fallen asleep in the car! Had that been a real turkey strutting on the steps of the Community Hall as they drove by or had she dreamed it? Sleepy and confused, she allowed her father to help her from the car.

Bright sunshine, streaming through the diamond-paned window, awakened her. Joanie could hear sounds from the kitchen below and realized the others were already up. That she could have slept so late on Christmas morning! This was the first time she had not wakened at the break of dawn. But then, in past years, she had gone to bed right after dinner because she had always been so impatient for the joys the morning promised. This year, having been considered old enough to attend the candlelight service and, sleepy as she was, enjoy a mince tart and hot chocolate afterward, it had been very late when she got to bed.

Now she jumped up, scrambled into her warm robe, and hurried down to the cosy kitchen. "Merry Christmas, Mother! Merry Christmas, Daddy! And Danny, Grandmother and Grandfather!" She ran around giving everyone kisses and hugs, both moist and enthusiastic. Danny streaked sticky fingers through her hair and laughed when she poked his tummy playfully. He was clad in the red-and-white striped pajamas Grandmother had made for him and he looked like one of the chubby little rascals in Joanie's copy of *The Night Before Christmas*. Not like a baby at all, Joanie thought, but awfully cute.

She turned away from Danny and said, "Now let's go look at the presents, everyone!" She started toward the living room, but her father called her back.

"This year," he said, "we are going to be civilized. You are old enough to wait and Danny is too young to know the difference, so we will get on the right side of a good breakfast first. Mother has it ready and we shouldn't let it get cold."

Joanie wailed, "Oh, Daddy, no! Why, some of the kids I know get to open their gifts on Christmas Eve! The twins do. Chris says they stay up until midnight and don't get up in the morning until almost lunch time and then they have brunch."

"Such a waste of daylight," Grandfather commented.

"Don't tease, Grandfather! I think it's a wonderful idea." She turned back to her father. "Ah, come on, Daddy — "

"We could have been halfway through breakfast already," Mr. Sanders pointed out with admirable patience, adding, "March! To the diningroom." He glanced at the popovers Mother was removing from the oven and added, "Those things are best eaten promptly."

Joanie loved popovers. And she knew that when Father spoke like that it was a waste of time to cajole or argue. She followed her grandparents to the diningroom, positive, however, that she wouldn't be able to eat a thing. But the popovers were airy light, the omelet fluffy and yellow with bits of chive in it and wreathed with tiny, sizzling sausages. No one could resist a breakfast like this. Joanie opened the red and green Christmas napkin by her plate and placed it on her lap. Then she drank her orange juice and helped herself to a generous portion of everything edible on the table.

Just as she had put the last of her fifth popover into her mouth, the doorbell rang. "I'll get it," she said, jumping up so hurriedly that her chair toppled backward and she almost went down with it.

By the time she reached the door, whoever had rung

141

the bell had already gone. Just one ring, for pity's sake! How impatient can a person be? And then, from near her feet, came a strange sound. She looked down at once and saw a huge red ribbon bow topping a good-sized, gaily-wrapped package. The strange noise was repeated and her heart began to beat a fast tom-tom rhythm. Could it be? Oh, she must hurry and find out! Just in case her guess was right, she lifted the big package with the utmost care and carried it back to the diningroom. There was no one there. Even Danny was gone from his high chair. Well, the living room, then. She almost tripped in her hurry to find the family.

There they all were, beside the Christmas tree, now lighted up as it had been last night. Everyone watched Joanie from the moment she entered the room. She set her package down on the floor, flopping down beside it, eager to look inside.

"Is this why we had to have breakfast first?" she asked, knowingly. "Because this is for me and it didn't arrive in time?"

"The tag reads 'Joanie,' doesn't it?" laughed her father. "Some things simply cannot be left overnight under a Christmas tree." He looked very pleased.

Joanie's trembling fingers were tearing off the wrappings. And suddenly — there he was! Around his neck was an enormous tag proclaiming his name to be Bernie. She picked up the puppy and pressed him to her rosy face. "Precious! Precious! Oh, I love you, I love you!" she crooned ecstatically.

"My, look at the size of those paws!" Grandfather said, impressed to the point of disbelief.

"That means he's going to become a very large dog,"

142

Joanie informed him with authority.

"Large! If that isn't the understatement of the day!" Grandfather laughed heartily.

"He's a Saint Bernard — aren't you, Bernie darling?" She stroked the puppy's toast-colored fur and dropped a kiss on the white spot between his eyes. "Look — he has dark brown around each eye and — oh, how snowy-white his little old fat tummy is! Daddy, what can he have to eat?"

"That 'little old fat tummy' tells me he's probably just eaten," Mr. Sanders guessed, taking Bernie from Joanie's arms to examine him. Then he gave the dog back to her. "Yes, he'll do. A beautiful animal, don't you think?"

"Gug, gug," Danny said, reaching chubby arms toward the puppy.

"He's my present, Danny. But you may play with him if you promise not to hurt him," Joanie announced possessively. "Look, see the lovely rocking horse Santa brought you, Danny?"

Danny continued reaching for the puppy and Joanie placed the furry ball in the baby's arms. Danny smiled angelically. Bernie yawned. Everyone else laughed.

Then Mr. Sanders asked Joanie, "Do you really think Bernie is the most beautiful dog in the whole world?"

"Oh, Daddy! I didn't believe any dog could be so perfect!"

"He was the finest of the litter — ask Jack Dawson," Mr. Sanders told her.

"Jack Dawson? Whatever would he have to do with

144

it? Or know about it?" Joanie was puzzled momentarily, but then she smiled. "Oh, yes, I remember now. Jack does have a Saint Bernard. Still — "

"Jack's dog is Bernie's mother."

"Oh. Oh! Well, for goodness' sakes!" Joanie exclaimed.

"From the litter they had planned to keep Bernie because he was such a beauty. But when I explained to him and his dad that I wanted the dog for you, Joanie, Jack immediately said I should take Bernie." Mr. Sanders spoke as though he was trying to tell Joanie something without putting it into words.

"Jack Dawson," Joanie mused. Another gift, really, even though Daddy had undoubtedly paid the asking price for Bernie. She inquired humbly, "How many puppies were there, Daddy?"

"Four. All very nice; thoroughbreds, of course. But this little guy — " Mr. Sanders patted Bernie fondly. Then he said, with a change of mood. "Well, folks, we have presents to open." He reached for the nearest one.

Joanie retrieved Bernie from Danny and said, "I don't really think I need anything else." But moments later she found her curiosity aroused when a gift wrapped in gold paper was dropped into her lap. The tag told it came from Grandfather. "Oh, how perfect!" she cried, discovering the gift to be a bright red leather collar and leash.

"It won't last that fellow too long," Grandfather prophesied. "He'll soon outgrow the thing. But after he's leash-trained, he probably won't need to be led around, he'll obey without it. Here, let's put the collar on." It seemed as though everyone wanted to get hold of

Bernie!

Watching her grandfather fasten the leash, Joanie observed, "They are really very smart dogs, aren't they?"

Another large package came her way and Mrs. Sanders said, "I suppose this, too, ought to have Bernie's name on it." The gift proved to be a basket-bed, complete with mattress.

"Bernie really rates, today," Joanie laughed, not caring that, so far, there was nothing more personal for her. But soon the usual books, new dress, paint set, and a real pearl to add to her add-a-pearl necklace came her way.

Meanwhile, of course, gifts were being opened by the rest of the family. One, opened unawares by Danny, brought everyone down upon him. He had the big box of chocolates, intended for passing around later on, opened and half-spilled on the floor around him. His small face, smeared with telltale smudges, wore a delighted smile. It seemed almost cruel to take the goodies from him! Joanie picked him up as he started to cry in protest. "There, little sweetheart, don't cry," she crooned.

"The pot-holders are lovely, Joanie. Did you weave them yourself?" Grandmother said, looking very pleased with the gift from her granddaughter.

"And my sachet! I love violet sachet most of all," her mother beamed, tucking Joanie's gift card back in the box.

Joanie set Danny down again and accepted the others' thanks with a modest, "I'm glad you like them."

The room was strewn with a rapidly mounting litter

146

of discarded wrappings. There were just a few more gifts left to be unwrapped. Most of them were Danny's and Joanie volunteered to open them for him. But suddenly there appeared to be no Danny in the room. Bernie too seemed to have vanished.

"Well, Danny can't be far away since he can't walk," Grandfather said, getting up from his chair to help find the little boy.

"Look! There he is — there they are — " Mrs. Sanders was pointing to the tree. At first unnoticeable, a tiny fist, relaxed from its hold on Bernie's collar, was suddenly seen by all. Danny was lying fast asleep on the floor behind the tree, Bernie cuddled beside him, drowsy and content.

"Aren't boys the very dickens, though!" Joanie sighed to her grandmother, as she watched her mother scoop up the sleeping baby.

"I'm afraid Christmas means little to Danny this year," his mother laughed, bearing him off to his crib, there to finish his midmorning nap in comfort.

Before they knew it, it was time to stuff the turkey and prepare all the other food that was to go into the makings of the holiday dinner. Joanie gave a fleeting thought to Archie and hoped that, wherever he was, he was having a wonderful time. She would have been proud to show him what a real family Christmas could be like. But perhaps he was enjoying one with the people his father had mentioned. She felt moved to close her eyes and whisper, "Please God, let Archie be having a good time."

Later, Joanie took Bernie for a walk in his new plaid jacket, his bright red leash fastened to the gleaming brass-and-leather collar. He looked like a prince of dogdom, Joanie thought with pride, though his behavior in the snow belied it. Apparently, Bernie loved snow better than anything. He rolled in it, he jumped in it, he ate it. He scampered around in the most unprincely fashion and shook himself frequently, so that Joanie was as covered with snow as was Bernie himself. She was wearing the new fur-lined gloves Grandmother had given her. Their luxurious warmth kept her comfortable even when she had to brush the snow from her clothing after tangling in Bernie's leash and falling headlong.

One or two other children appeared with brand new sleds, but most of the young people were remaining indoors, probably to play with new games and toys not meant for outdoor use. In satisfaction Joanie looked at Bernie and said, "I can play with *my* present, indoors or out, can't I, Bernie, old boy?" She failed to give a thought to the time when Bernie's ultimate size might keep him from indoor sport, when a house of his own in the back yard would be far more practical.

After a while, she began thinking of the turkey and the plum pudding and decided to go back home to see how far along dinner preparations might be. As she turned toward the house, however, she heard someone call her name. It was one of the girls in her Brownie troop, a Fifth Grader, Caroline Winters.

"Hi, Joanie! Oh, did you get *it* for Christmas? Oh, how perfectly darling!" Caroline picked up Bernie and cradled him in her arms. He licked her face enthusiastically. "His nose is cold!" Caroline giggled, snuggling her face in Bernie's fur. "And his coat's all wet," she added, though she didn't put the puppy down.

148

"A cold nose means a healthy dog," Joanie said, quoting her grandfather. She watched Bernie as he continued to lavish his affection upon Caroline and thought, "He certainly isn't a one-woman dog, yet!" But she smiled and was glad Caroline found him so admirable. Bernie could lick her friends' cheeks if he wished; he still belonged to her. In the long run, he would learn to know his mistress and she would be the one to enjoy his loyalty. All the dog stories she had read proved that.

Blissfully ignoring the damage Bernie might be doing to her nice jacket, Caroline said, "He likes me! He's a Saint Bernard, isn't he? How wonderful! He'll be able to pull your sled and — and — " She looked envious.

"And eat a ton of beef a day, Daddy says," Joanie laughed.

"Well, I love him, Joanie." Reluctantly Caroline returned the puppy to his mistress. "I wish — "

Joanie could guess what Caroline's wish was and she hoped that someday her friend would realize it. Then she hurried home. Dinner must be almost ready — and how hungry she was!

THIRTEEN

THE DAY AFTER CHRISTMAS Grandfather and Grandmother had to return home to their ranch in northern
California.

"Why must you leave so soon?" Joanie asked, having enjoyed all the extra attention only grandparents
can give.

"Chickens and pigs and cows need attention. They
don't fast or hibernate when the farmer wants a vacation," Grandfather explained.

"A neighbor kindly offered to take over for us while
we made this trip, so we can't impose further on his
generosity. We have a nice little arrangement with him
— when he goes on a brief fishing trip in the spring, we
keep an eye on his livestock," Grandmother further explained.

Early the next morning everyone arose, had a large
breakfast, and prepared for the trip to the airport. Then,
after seeing the visitors off, Daddy explained that he
had business in town and would meet Mother and
Joanie later in the day. Danny, of course, had been left
with the baby sitter.

"What shall we do, Mother?" Joanie asked, knowing that they could not return home without her father, since their car would be his only means of transportation home. The one bus that made the round trip from Briarcliff Lake would have left before Mr. Sanders expected to be free.

"Well, I have a little shopping to do — some I put off until we had Christmas out of the way," Mrs. Sanders answered.

"Oh, yes — and we have to exchange the snow suit for Danny, too. He eats too much!" Joanie said.

"A rather tiresome thing, exchanging merchandise the day after Christmas. I'm afraid we won't have any time to waste."

"But we'll have time for lunch?" Joanie loved this particular part of a shopping trip.

"Of course," her mother reassured her. "And how about shopping for a little informal get-together with your friends? We can have it tomorrow if you phone them this evening — nothing fussy, just fun."

"That's the best kind of a party," Joanie approved.

"Not a *party*," her mother chided.

"Can I invite the Brownie troop — all of them?"

"I was thinking perhaps your classmates — " Mrs. Sanders said, purposefully avoiding Joanie's eyes.

"A party for boys? *Mother!*"

"Not a party. And for girls too." Mrs. Sanders was turning in at Shipley's Department Store where the snow suit was to be exchanged.

Maybe some of the girls might like a mixed party, Joanie decided, but she was doubtful. And what on earth could they do? Even the food would have to be different. Girls liked fancy sandwiches and boys naturally would prefer hot dogs. She mentioned this as they stepped into the elevator.

Mrs. Sanders waited until they got out at the fourth floor before saying, "If you don't care for the idea, Joanie, we can forget it. I just thought — "

"Oh, no — " Joanie hastened to say. After all, she mustn't forget that some of the boys were being almost civilized in their behavior toward her lately. This would really be a very nice way of saying thank you, too, to the unknown gift-givers, and to Jack for letting her have Bernie. Come to think of it, Mother had come up with a very good idea.

Shopping for the project amounted to little more than buying several boxes of marshmallows for toasting over the fire. Rolls and meats could be purchased near home in the morning and there were lots of goodies left from Christmas to round out a fairly substantial luncheon for even the hungriest of guests.

At last Mrs. Sanders glanced at her wrist watch and exclaimed, "My goodness! Considering we had so little shopping to do, it certainly is very late! We'd better have lunch at once or they will be serving dinners only!"

Even in mid-afternoon the tearoom seemed to be crowded. "Exchangers, I suppose," Joanie murmured, when at last they were ushered to a tiny table for two. She scanned the menu hungrily and decided to have chicken a la king. Her mother was amused.

"It's probably left-over turkey," she teased, choosing a chef's salad for herself.

At a table close to the window, Joanie saw the twins with their mother. Surprised, she said, "Chris and Mark are over there, Mother — and how nice they look!"

152

She caught Mark's eye and he immediately drew his twin's attention to Joanie's presence. There was a moment of hand-waving and then the waitress came for the order. Seeing that the children recognized each other, the waitress said, "I think they are just finishing," which suggested that she might be wondering if Joanie and her mother had hoped to sit at the other table.

When she went away with their orders, Joanie giggled, "It would be like a preview, wouldn't it, having lunch with two of the boys today? No thanks!"

Mrs. Sanders smiled across the room at the twins' mother.

Soon their luncheon was served and Joanie gave all her attention to it. The next time she looked up, the twins were gone. This was a new idea to her — boys on a shopping trip with their mother. She wondered what they might have bought.

When the waitress returned with the check, she asked Joanie, "Are you going up to see the puppet show?"

"What puppet show?" Joanie inquired, instantly interested.

"A free one on the third floor — it is just about starting, I think. Every afternoon this week."

Mrs. Sanders glanced at her watch again. "We have forty-five minutes before we are to meet your father," she said, "so we might just as well look in on the show, dear." She thanked the waitress for telling them about it. "I suppose that's where the twins were going," she added.

When, a few minutes later, Joanie caught sight of the boys in the small auditorium, she thought, "I guess

153

boys actually like quite a lot of things girls like, come to think about it."

The show was delightful. Cleverly manipulated, the characters danced and "talked," performing a brief but charming version of *Hansel and Gretel*. Watching the wicked witch, Joanie could not help but think of Tommy Mason and she wished he could see the show. Perhaps, if she told him about it, he could get down to see it later in the week.

On the ride home, which was somewhat tedious after the day's activities, Joanie relaxed and thought about a number of things including, strangely enough, the witch of the puppet show. Despite her cruel behavior, something about the witch appealed to Joanie's sensitivity. After all, she reasoned, could a witch help having been born one? It must have been a dreadful fate — assuming, of course, that there really had been such creatures in days of old. And, oh dear, if there never had been any, think of all the lovely stories which might never have been written!

It was dark by the time they reached Briarcliff Lake. As they neared Lakeshore Drive, Mrs. Sanders said, anxiously, "Roger, do you smell smoke?"

Mr. Sanders sniffed, rolled down the window on his side and said, "Why, yes! Good heavens, Margaret, do you suppose — ?"

"Look over there, Daddy!" Joanie pointed towards the upper end of the road. There, dense black smoke mingled with a fire-like glow which most certainly could not be a sunset.

Mr. Sanders slowed down momentarily. Swirling smoke and greedy flames reached upward to light the

154

entire area with a frightening, eerie light. A fire engine had just come to a screaming halt and people were running from all directions. A patrol car blocked the entrance to Lakeshore Drive.

Slowly, the Sanders' car came alongside the patrol car and Mr. Sanders said, peering up the road, "It looks as though it might be the Polster place."

Shocked, Joanie cried out, "It is! It's Archie's!" Then she groaned, "Oh, Daddy!"

Regaining his composure a little, Mr. Sanders called to the patrol officer standing nearby, "We live up this way, officer. Any chance of getting through?" Mrs. Sanders cried out in sudden urgency, "We have a baby at home, sir!"

"Danny! Oh, Danny!" Joanie felt the icy fingers of fear clutch at her heart and she knew what her mother must be feeling. Danny! Dear God, let Danny be all right! Don't let the fire have reached where Danny is! She suddenly knew just how much she loved this little brother of hers. How she had always loved him, really. It was like letting go of a rope in a game of tug of war. Your hand smarted still — but oh, the joy of relaxing and letting go!

"The fire's concentrated in this spot for the time being," the officer explained reassuringly. "Of course, if a wind should come up — but the boys are already taking precautions beyond."

Mrs. Sanders sighed her relief and squeezed Joanie's hand. "But we may go through?" she asked the officer.

"Yes, ma'am. Just keep to the far left, Mr. Sanders, as you pass the fire area." The officer pulled his car to the side of the road to permit the passing of the Sanders' car. Then he moved in again immediately and Mr. Sanders, still driving at a snail's pace, leaned out to call back, "Anything I can do?"

"Since you live up here and are interested in the protection of your own place, you might join the volunteers. Ask the Chief," came the answer.

"Thanks — I'll do that." Mr. Sanders drove on as he said to his wife, "We'll water down the house the moment we get home, Margaret."

"Darling, I can do that alone," Mrs. Sanders insisted. "I'll turn on all the sprinklers and play the hose on the house itself. I know how much you want to get back — there. And do see how the Polsters are faring, will you?"

"They weren't expected back until this evening, late." Mr. Sanders offered this information with a sad shake of the head. "A fine return," he sighed.

Reaching their own home, Mrs. Sanders first checked inside the house to see that Danny was all right. The baby sitter, having heard the news of the fire, had gathered blankets and a few emergency supplies in case an evacuation should be necessary later. Danny was sleeping soundly in his crib. Mr. Sanders had already turned the car around and was on his way back to the fire. Telling Joanie she might help if she wished, Mrs. Sanders went outdoors and started the watering, though at the moment the house seemed to be in little danger.

Joanie wasn't much help. She found the faucets difficult to turn on, until suddenly one gave way unexpectedly and showered her with icy-cold water.

"Darling, I think you are tired. Why not just go in

and get to bed?" her mother suggested.

"Bed! Why, we haven't even had dinner! And — and anyway, it's preposterous, Mother! How could anyone go to *sleep* — "

Mrs. Sanders laughed, her tension relieved. "All right, dear. My goodness, it's been such a long day I was sure it must be close to midnight by now!" She surveyed Joanie's soaked clothes and said she should at least go and change.

Two hours later, Mr. Sanders returned home, looking grimy and tired. He was accompanied by the Professor and Archie. Their faces were white under smudges of soot and soil; their look of shock was heartbreaking to behold. They had arrived on the scene just in time to realize their home could not be saved. Everything they had in the house was destroyed along with the building itself.

"I'll make a pot of coffee," Mrs. Sanders said quietly.

Joanie, stealing a glance at Archie, found words too difficult to utter. What good would it do just to say she was sorry? She felt uncomfortable in the presence of such suffering, so she went to the kitchen to offer help there.

"Let's make a platter of sandwiches," Mrs. Sanders said, adding, "We haven't had anything to eat ourselves, for hours. No wonder your father looks wan." She began taking things from the refrigerator while Joanie got down a tray and cups and saucers. They took their time, however, giving the men a chance to wash up and to talk a little.

Presently, Archie came into the kitchen, smiling

157

apologetically. "May I have a drink of water, Mrs. Sanders?" he asked, rather pathetically, it seemed to Joanie.

"Of course! But we can do better than that! We have hot chocolate almost ready, and a pot of coffee for the grownups."

"C-can I help?" Archie asked, seeing the sandwich preparations in progress. "I'm pretty good at kitchen stuff. Dad lets me do the cooking lots of times — he prefers doing the cleanup. At least that's what he says, but maybe it's because I can't seem to get all the egg off the plates! Not that we eat eggs all the time, but when we do — " He continued to talk like this without interruption. Mrs. Sanders knew it was good for him to think of something besides the fire. She suggested he might apply mustard and mayonnaise to the sandwiches Joanie was putting together.

"You eat out quite a lot, don't you, Archie?" Joanie asked, sounding envious. She loved restaurants.

"We like it better at home," Archie confessed. "Only you can get awfully tired of fried chops and hamburger mix-up. That's what I call the stuff I make from hamburger and chili sauce and green peppers and canned corn or whatever there happens to be in the cupboard at the time. I'm learning, though. I can make pretty good pancakes. Dad does the flipping."

"That sounds like fun," Joanie said. Turning to her mother, she asked, "Is Archie going to sleep here tonight, Mother?" Immediately she wished she hadn't mentioned it in front of Archie. His face clouded and then, to her horror, Archie was weeping convulsively.

Mrs. Sanders laid down the knife with which she

had been slicing cold turkey. Going over to the boy, she put an arm about his shoulders and said, "Go ahead, Archie, cry all you want to. It wouldn't be human not to, at such a time."

Archie glanced at Joanie through his tears, and Joanie sensed the shame he was feeling that a girl should be seeing him cry. He started to brush his sleeve across his eyes but Joanie said, taking a cue from her mother, "Don't mind me, Archie. I know it's because of the poor fish. Anyone who cared so much about a pet — or pets — " It didn't sound quite right, but she supposed that was how Archie viewed the fish he owned.

Stoutly, honestly, Archie protested, "No, it isn't the fish. Well, yes, of course I feel badly about them too. But mainly it's Dad. All his manuscripts, all his work! I — I just don't know what he'll do — half a year's work."

Joanie caught her mother's eye and recognized the same admiration for Archie that she herself was feeling.

"If your father is anything like you, Archie dear, I'm sure you needn't worry too much about what he'll do." Mrs. Sanders patted the unhappy boy's shoulder and looked as though she too might break into tears momentarily.

Joanie was thinking, that wonderful aquarium! Yet here was Archie, thinking more of his father's loss than his own! Then, of course, there were all their clothes and the Christmas gifts they must have exchanged early so as not to have to carry them to the city and back. Everything they owned, practically, all burned in the fire! Yet Archie worried most over a manuscript.

It seemed very important to him that they understand why. "My father worked so hard," he said. "For three years he made notes and did research before we ever thought of coming up here. Then, one day, Dad said he'd found the perfect place where he might do the actual writing. It was so quiet, he said, and so — " Despair again colored the boy's words and he could not continue. Yet, after a brief silence, he squared his shoulders as he said, "Shall I carry out the tray for you, Mrs. Sanders?"

Archie, Joanie decided, was quite a boy.

The following morning, Joanie's first thought on awakening was of the get-together. Then all the events of the previous evening returned and she realized that last night there had been no thought of telephoning to invite her friends. And she remembered, too, that Archie was a house guest and that she'd better get downstairs just in case they were waiting breakfast for her.

"My, you certainly slept soundly," her mother greeted her. She was feeding Danny and said the men had already had breakfast and were on their way to the city where Professor Polster had business. "The fire insurance people, I think," she explained.

"Where's Archie?" Joanie asked, compassion tinging her voice.

"He insisted on bringing in logs for the fireplace," Mrs. Sanders replied. "What a nice boy he is." She finished feeding the baby and took him from his high chair. "Now, I'll fix something for you, Archie, and myself. Eggs or hot cereal?"

"Boys like both, don't they? I mean, Archie would no doubt like to have cereal *and* eggs and bacon. With

160

lots of toast. And I wouldn't want to embarrass him by eating like a bird, Mother. So I'll take a little of each, too." Joanie was looking about the kitchen as she talked. Where was Bernie? His basket, which had been placed in a warm corner, was empty.

Her question was answered almost at once as Archie came in from outdoors, looking rosy and cheerful. At his heels came the puppy who trotted over to his dish and sniffed hopefully. Archie laughed.

"We've had a good romp. I suspect he's hungry. A dog's a lot of fun, isn't it?" Archie's eyes were on the table, though he tried not to look too anxious. He went on, "There are quite a few logs just outside the door, Mrs. Sanders. Shall I carry them into the living room now, or — ?"

"Later will do, dear. Just sit down and we'll have our breakfast — I'm sure you must be starving by now." Mrs. Sanders put bowls of steaming oatmeal on the table and turned back to the stove to turn the sizzling bacon.

While they ate, Joanie mentioned the get-together. "I thought maybe we could call people right after breakfast," she said, hopefully.

"Darling, give me just one day to prepare!" her mother begged, with a little laugh. Then she added, "Anyway, I don't think you need worry too much about phoning — that phone has been ringing like mad ever since I got up this morning. People asking about you and your dad, Archie." She addressed the last directly to Archie.

"That was kind of them," the boy said, his face growing taut at mention of the tragedy.

"So I mentioned your little informal gathering to those who had any of your prospective guests in their homes. So far, they have all accepted. I told them it would be for lunch tomorrow."

After she had finished her breakfast, Joanie called Haystack and one or two others who would still be unaware of the luncheon plans. They accepted with enthusiasm. Everyone thought the party might help to cheer Archie and Joanie said she certainly hoped so.

When she was able to speak to her mother out of Archie's hearing, Joanie said, dispiritedly, "Mother, when the girls found out Archie was staying here, they asked all kinds of questions. They seem to think I should know all the Polsters' business just because — well — anyway, nothing would keep them from coming. It's positively revolting!"

"Oh, it's only natural. Wouldn't you be a little curious if it were some other girl in your position?" Mrs. Sanders asked.

Joanie shook her head, positive she would not. Her mother continued, "Once they see Archie again and discover he looks exactly as he did the last time they saw him, their curiosity will dwindle."

"I don't mean they aren't sorry for him," Joanie added, just as the telephone rang once more. Her mother hastened to answer it and Joanie finally had a chance to pick up Bernie and cuddle him for a while. "Everyone calling to offer something," she murmured to the sleepy animal, "from blankets to dishes. But they have no house to put them in. Oh, Bernie — " She brushed away the tears. It wouldn't do for Archie to find her crying.

The fathers returned in the late afternoon, looking

as if they had accomplished a few things. Mr. Sanders said the insurance people had been most considerate, though of course it would take more than consideration to solve the Professor's problems. The latter had decided to reopen the apartment he and Archie had occupied in the city. Fortunately he had a five-year lease on it, with three years still to go.

"I could have subleased, but I thought it wiser just to close up the apartment for the year we were to spend up here. A good thing, as it has turned out," Doctor Polster said, ruefully. "We can move into it immediately. There are sufficient furnishings, though all of our personal effects were up here."

"We will hate to see you leave here, Doctor," Mrs. Sanders said, "but of course you have no alternative, I know."

"I hate to go. However, I will have access to the University library and I believe I have carbons of a few of my notes at the apartment. With these, I shall endeavor to begin again on my book. A man has to have something — " The Professor sounded so wistful that Joanie felt a lump rise in her throat.

"Doctor Polster, do you mean that Archie must go back to the city? That he won't be coming back to our school — ever?" Joanie suddenly cried out in a shocked tone.

Mrs. Sanders seemed surprised at Joanie's outburst and, after a glance at her husband, she said, "We would be happy to keep Archie here with us until the end of the present semester. If you can spare him, that is. After all, there are only a few more weeks after the holidays."

Father and son exchanged inquiring looks. Archie said, "It would be up to you, Dad."

"I'd miss you very much, son," his father replied, adding, "but I do think it would be a good idea for you to finish the semester here. It is more than kind of Mr. and Mrs. Sanders to make the offer." He turned to Mrs. Sanders and asked, "Would you give me a little time to consider it?"

FOURTEEN

THE FOLLOWING DAY WAS one Joanie would never forget. She arose early to help with the preparations for her "little shindig," as her father called it, and to keep an eye on Danny while her mother went to the market for the necessary food. The men seemed to have business which took them down the hill once more and Archie again offered to bring in logs and to do anything else he could to help. Joanie thought it was almost like having a big brother in the house and she found that she rather liked the idea. Of course, brothers quarrelled and teased, she knew, but still, if Archie was permitted to stay with the Sanders for the next few weeks, she thought there was little likelihood of his becoming that brotherly!

At precisely eleven-thirty, the doorbell rang, announcing the arrival of the first luncheon guests. "Good heavens! Already?" Joanie wailed in mock anguish, as she hurried to the door. She hadn't expected anyone until twelve o'clock.

Archie had disappeared. Probably getting cleaned up, Joanie thought, remembering that he had no fresh clothes to change into and would have to wear the ones he had worn since leaving the city to come back to

Briarcliff Lake.

She opened the door wide and stepped back in surprise. Tommy Mason and the Riley twins, Chris and Mark, stood on the porch, each boy with an object in his hands, none of which seemed appropriate to bring to a luncheon. Tommy carried two, a shining new fishing pole and a wicker fishing basket. Tommy and his fishing! Joanie guessed he just wanted to show off his new equipment.

Chris bore a bright red pogo stick and Mark carried a pair of odd-looking shoes with springs attached to the soles.

Tommy said, "We came early because — well — because we brought stuff for Archie."

Feeling some chagrin, Joanie smiled quickly and said, "Oh. Oh! Well, come on in — I'll call him." Her eyes were on three pairs of galoshes, all heavily caked with snow and mud. Mother's spanking-clean floors! But, surprisingly, the boys began immediately to remove the overshoes and to set them in a neat row on the porch. Chris remarked, "Mom told us to — "

"Yeah," Mark added, "Mom said your mother had fancy rugs."

"And isn't used to boys racing all over them," Chris finished for his twin.

Tommy explained, as the three boys stepped inside, "We all heard how Archie's presents got burned in the fire, so — " He set his offerings down on the hall table.

"But — these are all new things!" Joanie exclaimed, calling to her mother and to Archie to "come see what the boys have brought!"

Archie was stunned by this display of generosity.

166

"But Tommy, didn't you ask for a new fishing pole for Christmas?" he inquired suspiciously.

Tommy fidgeted. "Yeah. But gee, I already have one — a real good one, too," he lied, while Joanie tried to understand how a boy like Tommy could suddenly show such kindness. He was making a real sacrifice. Tommy loved fishing.

And the twins, one at a time, yet in the same amazingly identical voices that made one look to see which one was speaking, said, "Gosh, we got so much stuff for Christmas — we don't even have time to play with everything! Honestly!"

The doorbell rang again. This time Bobby, Damon, and Jack stood waiting on the doorstep, also laden with gifts. Jack looked a little anxious as he said, "I hope Archie'll like these — they aren't as fancy as the ones he had." He was holding a large glass bowl containing an assortment of tropical fish.

"Oh, Jack, he'll love you!" Joanie cried, excitedly.

Jack blushed and muttered, "That's all right — " He pointed to Damon who had a jacket over one arm. "Look at what Damon brought! Real leather! *It's* for Archie, too!"

Damon seemed self-conscious and only smiled at Joanie.

Bobby, looking terribly eager, said, "See that bike by the fence? I got it for Christmas and I'm giving it to Archie on account of he has nothing left — " His face was red, showing the embarrassment he felt at his own generosity. He shuffled his feet as he added, "Anyway, my old one's pretty good still. And I'm kinda used to it."

Joanie was ready to cry and had to swallow before

she could say anything.

Archie, of course, was too overcome for words. When at last he could speak, he remonstrated with the boys for being what he considered far too kind. But he was assured, over and over again, that it was quite all right, that even their parents approved.

A third summons to the door revealed Eric, all alone. "Hello, Joanie, am I late?" he asked.

"Goodness, no. The boys all seemed to want to get here early — lunch won't be on the table for at least half an hour." She noted that Eric's arms were full. She laughed, "Don't tell me, let me guess. They are for Archie! Come in — "

As he removed his boots, Eric told her he had stopped by James's house. "He has a bad cold and his mother thought it wouldn't be fair to the rest of us for him to come. But he sent these." Eric indicated two packages. Then he followed Joanie to the living room where the others were gathered.

As Archie unwrapped the gifts brought by Eric, he said, "I seem to be getting more presents than I got in the first place — before the f-fire — " He stopped speaking and there was a moment's silence, for everyone knew the difficulty Archie must be having in controlling himself. Then, as the wrapping was peeled from one of the boxes, Archie smiled with pleasure. "Well! I sure need *this!*" he said, holding up a bright red shirt. "Say — ! There are two! A blue one *and* the red! And — gosh! A pair of blue jeans! Oh, thank you, Eric, a million times!"

"They are from James," Eric corrected Archie. Then he offered another package and said, "This is from me, Arch. With all your books burned up, you will have to start a new collection and my father thought these — "

After opening this particular package, Archie sighed with pleasure. There were three volumes, profusely illustrated, one bearing the title, *Stories From Greek Mythology;* another, *Tales From Shakespeare*, and the third, *Aesop's Fables*. This was absolutely too much, Archie protested, delighted with the books. They were brand new, undoubtedly from among Eric's own Christmas gifts, as the gifts of all the others had been.

Just then Mrs. Sanders announced, "I think I hear some girls on the porch, Joanie."

Joanie once again ran to the door. The girls had all come in a group. Haystack, staring down at all the galoshes lined up near the door, remarked flippantly, "My, the boys couldn't wait to get here!"

Joanie silenced her with a finger to her lips and then, in a whisper, told the newcomers what had happened. "Oh dear," moaned Haystack, "I didn't know we were supposed to bring — "

"But you weren't. This was the boys' own idea. Can you imagine!" Joanie still seemed astonished.

"Their own presents?" one of the other girls asked, disbelief coloring her words.

"Well, we could hardly have done the same," Caroline Winters laughed. "I'm sure Archie wouldn't know what to do with a taffeta dress or a sewing kit!"

"Come on into the diningroom — lunch is about ready," Joanie said, putting an end to the girls' comments.

Mrs. Sanders told the children that they were to help themselves from the buffet where baskets of hot

170

rolls, bowls of potato chips and pickles, platters of hamburger patties and frankfurters awaited their pleasure.

Starting on her second hot dog, Haystack said, "Well golly, you fellows, it sure was nice of you to be so nice to Archie — "

"Aw, forget it," Bobby muttered, through a big bite of hamburger.

Archie was looking uncomfortable and Joanie thought Haystack might have shown a little more tact.

Mark said, quietly addressing Haystack, "If it had been you, well — golly — anybody'd do the same."

But, looking around at the girls' faces, Joanie wondered. Would they do the same for one of their number? She wasn't sure. Noting their expressions at the moment, she thought they were all too awed and impressed to tell Mark he was right. Of course, the boys' act *had* seemed incredible, so perhaps the girls, too, under the same circumstances — ? No, she simply didn't think they would have given up their very best presents as the boys had done. To herself she admitted she might have given up her *second-best* present, but not her *best*. Her best had been Bernie! Boys were certainly peculiar. Take Jack, for instance. He must have loved Bernie. Which reminded her, "Jack, I want to say thanks for letting Daddy buy Bernie for me — I've never seen such a wonderful dog! I'll take the best care of him."

"Well, I knew that — " Jack grinned.

"Boys and girls, if you have finished here, we can go into the living room and toast marshmallows," Mrs. Sanders said a few moments later.

Each guest was provided with a long pointed stick on which to spear the marshmallows. Perhaps it was the tantalizing aroma of toasting marshmallows that brought the puppy, Bernie, on a tour of investigation. Close on his heels came Danny, fresh from his nap and glowing with pleasure at the sight of so many young people in the house.

It wasn't long before a full-scale roughhouse was in session. Joanie was surprised to see that boys not only liked dogs, they liked babies equally well. At least, they liked Danny! It was all too obvious the way they enjoyed playing with the little fellow, tickling him, tossing him around, making him laugh until his mother finally decided it was time for him to settle down.

Bernie, too, came in for a share of the boys' romping and teasing. It wasn't until one or two of the boys forgot themselves to the point of jumping over the furniture that Mrs. Sanders suggested perhaps they might like to play outdoors for a while. The boys, Joanie decided, were back in character, halos askew, their boisterous behavior once again taking over.

"Yeah! Say, Archie, why don't you try out the pogo stick?" Chris suggested, his eyes lighting up.

"Don't you think it's a little to slushy out there for pogo jumping?" Mrs. Sanders said, eyeing doubtfully the bright new stick.

Just then Eric looked at the clock and said he had to be leaving, he'd promised to help his father address some envelopes before dinner. Looking around at the others, he said, apologetically, "But don't let me break up the party, kids."

"If it wasn't so sloppy outside, we could perhaps have a baseball game," Joanie said.

"Boys against girls," one of the girls put in, sounding as though she expected the girls to win.

"Good thing it *is* sloppy out — we'd sure beat you," Tommy remarked confidently.

Suddenly Joanie remembered. "When we lived in the city, my father was the boys' football coach!" she announced.

"Gosh! Honest, Joanie?" It was Mark who spoke but all the boys were properly impressed.

Joanie nodded.

"How about baseball?" Jack asked.

"He's good at that too," came the proud reply.

Inspired, Chris said, "Say! Do you think maybe your father would coach us, Joanie? I mean, we could have a Little League team if we had a coach. Jack's real good, and so is Mark, for a lefty."

"Daddy could coach anything!" Joanie could not let this moment of glory be skipped over lightly. She promptly took it upon herself to offer her father's services. "I'll tell him as soon as he comes home that you want him," she promised.

Mrs. Sanders suggested, rather pointedly, "Wouldn't it be better just to ask him if he wants to do it, Joanie?"

"Yeah, Joanie — you ask him," Tommy said, tying his scarf snugly around his neck.

The phone rang again and Mrs. Sanders went to answer it. When she returned to the children, who were in the hall donning outdoor clothing now, she said, "That was your mother, Chris and Mark. She thinks you ought to get started on your way home — it gets dark so early."

Reluctantly, Chris said, "Aw, gee," but brightened when, one by one, the other guests decided that they too

173

ought to be leaving. Caroline put it best into words by saying, "We were having such a lovely time we had no idea it was getting so late, Joanie."

The exodus began. "Goodbye, Joanie — had a wonderful time — " And soon the house was back to normal again.

Mr. Sanders and the Professor arrived home in time for dinner, the latter appearing to be in better spirits. Mrs. Sanders asked how things were coming along.

"Just fine. The insurance investigator has checked the damage and there won't be any trouble settling the claim," Professor Polster told her. "Naturally, nothing can be done about the personal treasures, which we shall miss more and more as times goes by."

"Like Archie's fish?" Joanie asked, her eyes wide in sympathy. "Will the insurance people buy more fish for him?"

"I'm afraid not," the Professor answered ruefully, giving his son a passing smile of regret.

"Or your manuscript," Archie reminded his father.

"Yes, sir," Mr. Sanders commented, "I suppose one must be prepared to come out the loser in spite of insurance."

"Oh, it will be better than nothing at all," the Professor insisted with a little smile. "For a moment there, watching those flames licking away like a greedy dragon, I guess I came close to panic. You know, I couldn't remember if I'd paid my last insurance premium!" He laughed with the others as Mr. Sanders said something about "the absent-minded professor."

Then, more seriously, Professor Polster went on,

174

"I do feel somewhat disturbed about all the gifts Archie received today. They are far too much." He paused thoughtfully, before adding, "I'm sure the donors were all sincere, of course, but — " He turned toward Archie. "We ought to make sure, son, that these young people didn't act on sheer impulse and are not already regretting their sacrifice. To think that a boy could willingly give up such a treasure as that — " He indicated Tommy's fishing pole. "It seems incredible."

Archie, his gaze upon the floor, murmured with conviction, "Dad, if you'd seen them! I'm sure they meant it — and still do. But of course, if you think I ought to return the things, why — "

Glancing at Archie, Joanie thought he looked just the way she felt the time that some tiresome character had stuck a pin in a balloon she was enjoying. She burst out, "Oh no, Doctor Polster! It isn't just Archie who'd be hurt, I know. The boys would too. You can't do a thing like that!"

"No, I suppose not," the Professor admitted, giving Joanie a gentle smile.

A moment later, Mr. Sanders said to Joanie, "We can mark this day on the calendar as the one when the horrible toads turned into fairy princes, eh, Princess?"

Doctor Polster asked, "Isn't Joanie the only girl in Fourth Grade?"

"It's been rather rough on her," her mother nodded.

"Rough? Why, Mother, it's been wonderful! I mean, our Fourth Grade is the most marvelous Fourth Grade in the world!"

"And pretty soon you'll be leaving it," her father reminded her. "I believe you are still maintaining the good grades — "

"No!" Joanie interrupted. Then, more quietly, she added, "I mean, yes. The grades are fine. I mean no, I won't be leaving — oh — " She wasn't making much sense, she thought, as she turned to her mother in some dismay, her eyes lowered.

"You sound a little confused," Mr. Sanders commented.

"What I mean is, Daddy, I like it in Fourth. And they all like me, I know they do. I mean, I need to toughen up a bit, but — well — do you think maybe you could start calling me Jo? That's short for Joanie, you know." She raised her eyes slowly and saw that her parents were finding her words difficult to understand. Her father actually groaned.

"After all the tears! And the hard work! To say nothing of the difficult times you have given your mother and me!" He shrugged his broad shoulders in a way which meant, "I give up! I simply give up!"

Mrs. Sanders wailed, "And she wants us to call her Jo! Roger, I won't have it! I simply won't!" She looked at the puzzled Professor and told him, "All we ever asked of her was a little tolerance for the boys. We didn't expect her to do a complete turnabout!" She sounded quite distraught.

Mr. Sanders looked bewildered as he said, "Well, Margaret, don't look at me as though all this was my idea."

The Professor and Archie sat in silent discomfort. Neither quite understood what was taking place. Both looked as though they were considering leaving until this little family matter could be settled. Then Mr.

Sanders caught the Professor's eye and he grinned.

"Unless you should some day become the father of a girl child, Doctor, you will never, but *never*, understand what is going on here. As a matter of fact, even if you do have a daughter, you may never — " he gave up, shaking his head slowly.

Joanie turned imploring eyes his way, saying earnestly, "Daddy, have you forgotten how mad you got when I said I hated boys? Honestly, I just don't understand parents, I really don't." She turned her eyes heavenward and sighed heavily.

"*She* doesn't understand *parents!* Oh, my gosh!"

Joanie looked to Archie for the support she needed. He had remained silent throughout all this, but now he seemed to feel it was safe to speak up.

"Oh, we do like her, sir! We think Joanie's just about tops. I mean, at first some of the boys thought it might upset everything, you know — "

"Yes, Daddy, that's the way it was. And you must admit, I was a bit of a pill, too, in the beginning," came Joanie's amazing confession.

"Only in the beginning?" her father prompted.

"All right. All along, then. But everything's changed now, Daddy, and I — "

"Would you still want to remain in Fourth if there should happen to be a few other girls there too?" her father asked. "Is it because you like the boys so much now, or that you like the distinction of being the only girl in the room?"

"Daddy!"

"I have a reason for asking, Joanie," Mr. Sanders told her, "so will you try to answer, please?"

"I like the boys. Who wouldn't, when they've all been so wonderful? And that's the truth, Daddy, cross my heart." After a pause she asked, "Why is it so important for you to know?"

"Well — and this is confidential — I happened to hear something interesting today. If you two promise not to say anything to the other children before Mrs. Westcott has a chance to announce it to the entire studen body, I will tell you."

"Me too, Mr. Sanders?" Archie asked, looking pleased.

"Yes."

"We promise — don't we, Archie?" Joanie was only too eager to hear the news her father had to tell.

"Well, the schoolhouse at Spring Valley has recently been condemned by the County Building and Safety Department as being unsafe for further use. So, with the new semester, Spring Valley will unify with Briarcliff Lake. The Spring Valley children will come by bus to our elementary school. Fortunately, we have room for them. It will mean five or six new pupils, on an average, for each grade. It is reasonable to expect that there will be at least two or three girls entering Fourth Grade. So you see, Joanie, you haven't much longer to enjoy your present distinction of being the only one." Mr. Sanders gave Joanie a level look, adding, "There is still time, if you feel you want to try fifth-grade work."

Joanie was stunned. Archie shared her dismay until she reminded him that he would not be affected by the change, since he would be leaving the district in a few weeks anyway. He said, dolefully, "I sure will miss all you kids up here."

178

Mr. Sanders said, "How about it, Joanie? Why waste all your hard work? You can go into Fifth and feel proud of your accomplishment."

"Daddy! For goodness' sake, don't you understand? The boys are my friends. I don't want to have to start all over making new ones. Why is it so important to go into Fifth?" Joanie asked irritably.

Her mother said, "Does it really matter, Roger, now that it doesn't seem urgent to Joanie herself? All we really want is for her to be happy. It isn't as though she were behind at all and, in fact, I doubt she ever will be again. She seems to have established fairly good study habits, you know."

Cheered by her mother's championing of her cause, Joanie begged, "Then it's all right? I may stay in Fourth? It's all as good as settled, Daddy?"

"You may remain in Fourth for sixty years if you want to," her father suddenly exploded, evidently still unable to accept this sudden about-face in his daughter. Then he turned to the Professor and asked if he wouldn't like to take a nice long walk with him. "Trees don't change. Frogs and butterflies don't change. Rabbits don't change. Only — "

"Oh, but you're so wrong, Daddy!" his daughter exclaimed. "Maybe not the pine trees so much, except for growing taller. But apple trees do! My goodness, they blossom and they bear fruit and then, in winter, they are quite bare. And as for frogs! Heavens, Daddy, have you forgotten they come from tadpoles?"

Archie grinned and added, "Yes, sir! And consider butterflies — I mean, maybe *they* don't change, but caterpillars do! As a matter of fact, everything in nature changes, Mr. Sanders."

"Anyway, it's dark in the woods," Joanie began and then stopped, realizing that all her father was trying to do was to make it clear to all concerned that never, never in a hundred years, would he understand his young daughter. Suddenly she gave a gay laugh. "What you mean is, I'm just a fickle pickle, eh, Daddy?"

Mr. Sanders grinned, back to his good-humored self once more. "That's better than being an old pickle puss, at that," he grinned, and tweaked the tip of her nose.

A surge of affection for her father swept through Joanie. He was so nice! It was a good thing he had a little boy. She was very glad about that, now. Boys were the *nicest!* Well, most of the time they were. It was Danny's sudden entrance that caused her to qualify her opinion, for he was covered from head to foot with maple syrup. He was licking his hands and wearing a most innocent and endearing smile. But the most amazing part of it was, he was walking! All alone and staggering mightily, but on his own two feet! Who cared that he'd been into the bottom cupboard, probably leaving it a shambles? Danny was walking!

Joanie beat everyone else to Danny's sturdy, determined little form and swooped him into her arms. "Sweetums! I love you! Love you! Hey — for goodness' sake, take your sticky little paws out of my hair! Danny! Oh, you little — you little — " Laughing, she handed her brother over to her mother's waiting arms.